T

To JILL & JUSTIN,

Widdershins

EVE
LESTRANGE

Eve Lestrange

To

Silk & Dustin,

3/5

Lestrange

Widdershins
Copyright 2009 Eve Lestrange
All Rights Reserved
Second Printing November 2014
ISBN 9781492943228
ISBN: 1492943223

Written By Eve Lestrange
Cover by Jose Pardo
Authors photo by Nancy Poyssick

Widdershins
By Eve Lestrange

Dedication

To Mom, who always encouraged me to write.
E.

1

elcome to a meeting of ink and paper meant to chronicle the life of one who is damned. By no means is this a confession or a warning. I have already confessed everything to those responsible for my imprisonment and now await my journey to the gallows. I must say I feel no remorse or guilt for any of my actions because I do not feel I have done wrong. I will meet death with head held high and hand extended to accept his eternal dance.

My name is Christina LaFage and I die as a member of the wealthy upper class but I have not always been so. I was born unto poor parents in a small village outside Paris. As a child I would often see members of the nobility pass through our village wearing fine silks and jewels, riding on magnificent stallions or in gilded carriages. As I watched them I always felt I belonged with them rather than the poor peasants of the village.

I asked my mother as a child of six if we would ever be members of the nobility and have fine clothes and ride in gilded carriages to which she replied, "Young child, you have much of the world to learn. We are of the poor peasant class and of that class we shall remain." But somehow I knew that another destiny awaited me.

Now our village had always been very religious but I never quite understood prayer. We prayed yet we were still poor; we prayed before meals but always had little to eat. I had asked my mother why we prayed because it seemed we were never heard. "God does not grant earthly riches but rewards us in Heaven," was her reply.

"But what about while we are here, why should we suffer so?" I asked.

"You are too smart for your own good and too young to worry about such things," she replied. This was not a sufficient answer for me, but she would discuss it no further and told me that I should pay more attention at mass.

We attended mass faithfully but quite frankly I found the whole ceremony rather tedious. Colorless rituals performed by celebrants with no emotion did not appeal to me at all, but when I criticized or questioned the ritual, I was sent to my room and told to pray for forgiveness, but my prayers were empty and unemotional.

I had begun to feel estranged from everyone and a bit saddened that I did not feel the same way everyone else did at mass. They seemed to draw joy and fulfillment from an experience which left me confused and unmoved. The only time I did enjoy going to church was when a member of our village had passed away and the church became a home to the deceased while a requiem mass was being performed. I held a profound interest in the funeral rite and the ceremony where the deceased was laid to rest. I found solace in the somber mood and the melancholy dirges the congregation sang as the lifeless star of the production lay at the front of the congregation. The forlorn rhythms of the music aroused something deep within me so much that I actually felt as if I was part of the dismal hymns and chanting. The rhythms would often linger in my memory and I would sing them to myself as we accompanied the deceased to the churchyard for interment. As I would watch the body being lowered into the ground, I wondered what the other occupants of the cemetery looked like after being buried for so long. I had never seen a decayed body and could only imagine what a decomposed corpse looked like. I tried to envision how they looked in life as I read the inscriptions on the tombstones and imagined their flesh withering away eventually exposing bare bones.

I loved the time I spent in the churchyard, especially when no other living soul accompanied me. I felt at home in the solitude among the weathered tombstones and stone crypts that protruded from the ground as if they had sprung forth from the very bowels of the earth.

My parents, unfortunately, had perceived my churchyard visits as an unhealthy pastime for their only child and put an end to my churchyard wanderings. They instead encouraged me to play with the other children, which I reluctantly attempted and found their interests were quite different from my own. They had no interest in the beauty of the churchyard or the inscriptions on the tombstones of the long dead. I was often the subject of their ridicule and taunting which I pretended not to be bothered by, but the expression behind the defiant mask that I wore was one of sadness and rage that I not only felt toward my tormentors, but also toward myself. As much as I tried to fit into their world, something deep within me would not allow it, but I managed to keep up the charade in public despite my true feelings. I tried to show interest in childish games and church rituals but I secretly longed for the solitude and mystery of the churchyard.

I maintained the appearance of an ordinary child for a few years until I could stand it no more. All the lying to myself and striving to be accepted by others that I did not even care for began to eat away at me. I began to secretly visit the churchyard at night when my parents and the rest of the village were asleep. I preferred the church empty and dark; it seemed to make the churchyard beyond more mysterious and inviting. My nightly visits to the churchyard revived my spirit and melted my sadness if only for a while; during the day I continued the charade of an ordinary child. My nightly wanderings were a closely guarded secret, but as much as I enjoyed my perverse little secret, I still did not feel as though I belonged in the village. I would ponder this as I sat in the solitude of the churchyard and try to think of a way out but I was only a child, where else could I go? I had no money and my parents had none to give me.

During one of my visits, on a particularly blustery night, I sensed something different about the churchyard. I couldn't quite figure out what it was, everything looked the same, yet there seemed to be something different in the air that was just beyond my perception and as the wind rushed through my hair and my eyes closed, I heard it whisper, "Christina," and my eyes quickly opened and scanned the churchyard for the intruder but saw nothing. I attributed it to my imagination and the rustling wind and that would have comforted me had it not come again, this time louder and more distinct. My heart began to pound and the palms of my hands became sweaty as I bolted from the churchyard toward the safety of my own bed. I spent a nervous night wondering if my secret had been exposed and what my parents would do if they found out. The morning found me still nervous and exhausted from lack of sleep but not a word was said to me about my nightly wanderings, much to my relief. But if the whisper in the darkness I heard was not that of a watcher, then who or what had been in the churchyard? I awaited nightfall with great anticipation and returned to the churchyard listening intently for the phantom whisper. The wind came, rustling through the leaves of the ancient trees and over the weathered tombstones but it did not carry with it the strange voice I longed to hear. However, the voice did not come and I was disappointed, but I still felt that something in the churchyard was different. I sensed a presence, yet there was no one else in the church-yard. I was not frightened by what I sensed but felt rather comfortable and secure by the unseen force that seemed to watch over me. Still, I continued to exercise caution on my nightly sojourn as the years passed and I grew into young adulthood. I never heard the voice again, but the vigilant presence remained, ever watchful over me. At times I would of-ten speak to the unseen presence when I felt it very strongly throughout the churchyard. At first I would speak of my fondness for the church-yard and the feeling of serenity it gave me, but as I became at ease with the presence I would confide my deepest desires and frustrations toward my parents, the village and our unbearable poverty. I felt as if someone was really listening to me and on certain nights when I felt particularly downhearted I could swear that I felt phantom arms wrap around me giv-ing the comfort that I needed.

One night while sitting next to a particularly ancient crypt, I caught sight of something protruding from the earth. It was a small object, and

I probably would not have seen it had it not been for a very bright moon. As I picked it up and examined it more closely, I realized it was a fragment of bone that had been under the earth for some time, but whether animal or human I could not tell. I admired the texture and shape of the bone fragment and regarded it a favorable omen. Upon arriving home that night, I fashioned the bone fragment into a necklace that I kept hidden underneath my clothes as a constant reminder of the churchyard that had become my refuge from the mundane world of poverty and boredom. However, my secret visits to the churchyard were abruptly halted when my father discovered me sneaking into the house one summer night on the eve of my fourteenth birthday. "Where have you been, Christina?!" he furiously questioned me, "And who were you with?!" He thought I had gone to meet a lover and he probably would have preferred that assumption to the answer I gave him, "I was alone . . . in the churchyard."

"The churchyard!" He scolded, "I have told you before you have no business in a place for the dead!"

"But it's peaceful there . . . " I protested before being cut short by my father's accelerated anger followed by a hard slap across my face.

"Strange things transpire in places of the dead that the living are not meant to behold!" he shouted.

"The churchyard is no place for a young woman, Christina," my mother broke in as she entered the room. I was angry, but I dared not say anything else about the churchyard, especially about the presence that I felt there. Tears filled my eyes as I stormed past my father toward my room, but I didn't get very far as he grabbed my arm and yanked me toward him revealing the necklace I had fashioned from the bone fragment. "And what is this?!" he angrily asked as he ripped the trinket from my neck.

"I, I found it in the churchyard," I nervously answered.

"The devil has a hold on you, Christina! This is an evil talisman!" he shouted as he threw it into the hearth. "Burn it, Marguerite," he strongly ordered my mother. I started to object, but stopped myself to avoid another surge of my father's anger. I kept silent as my parents ranted and raved about the churchyard being an evil place and how my soul was in jeopardy. I had never perceived the churchyard as an evil place and could not understand why anyone would see it as such. How could a place so peaceful be evil? My confusion over my parent's concern quickly turned to shock as my father announced, "Christina, I think it would be better for you if we sent you to the convent." The convent! Thoughts of a sheltered existence locked away in a cold chamber, kneeling in prayer swarmed through my mind as my eyes widened and my jaw dropped in horror. I would have to act fast if I was to avert imprisonment in a convent. "Father, please," I tearfully begged as I knelt in front of him. "I did not realize the danger I put my soul into, I never meant to commit sin. I am so sorry and I swear I will never visit that evil place again!" I lied . . . and hated myself for it, but I could see no other way out of life in a convent.

"Places of the dead are where the devil holds court, Christina," he affirmed as he knelt beside me, lifted my head and stared into my tear-filled eyes, "Are you sure you were alone and no one came to you?"

"I swear I was completely alone, no being of flesh or spirit came to me," I cried. I begged and pleaded with my parents until dawn and had ultimately won them over and my father had finally relented, "Very well, Christina, however I still think the convent would serve you better, but you seem penitent and I will give you another chance. But be warned, if you falter, I will have no choice but to send you to the convent."

"Thank you, father," I sobbed, but it was not out of remorse that I sobbed; it was for the loss of my place of solitude and the watchful presence that comforted me. My sorrow satisfied my parents and they did not need to know the real reason for my anguish.

I kept my word and stayed away from the churchyard, silently apologizing to the presence that had watched over me. My behavior seemed to pacify my parents who took me to church regularly and made sure my attention stayed focused on the mass.

But secretly, I still yearned to get away, to be free of my parents and the poor village that was my home. It was one particular sermon one Sunday that roused my attention and set a plan into motion. The priest spoke of the power of prayer being able to overcome anything no matter how grave the situation may be. I had tried prayer before to no avail, but maybe I was not praying hard enough. Maybe if I prayed hard enough God would send a rich nobleman for me to marry who could give me all of the finer things that I longed for and provide an escape for me. For three years I prayed; I prayed in the Church, I prayed in the wooded grove outside the village and I would pray every night before drifting into slumber. I thought as a young woman of seventeen my prayers would soon be answered. I even rejected the attentions of some of the young men of my village, despite my curiosity and growing desire for a lover in the hope that my prayers would be answered. Another year had passed and my praying had still gone un-answered and the seeds of doubt were being sown.

One morning while feverishly praying in the wooded grove I began to feel a strange presence around me that I had not felt in years but had never forgotten, only it was slightly different, like someone . . . *watching* and I heard a voice. A voice that I had heard only once, years ago in the solitude of the churchyard. It softly whispered my name and my heart beat furiously as my eyes shot open and I looked up to find standing be-fore me an older woman with milk-white skin and raven-black hair, very finely attired with an air of aristocracy. "What are you doing, child?" she gently asked.

"P-praying," I sheepishly relied.

"Praying," she said, "And to what gods do you pray to?"

"Why, I pray to the only god, the Christian God," I replied. With that the woman threw her head back with laughter and then asked, "And what do you ask of this God?" "Well, it is a very personal request, Madame, that I would rather not relate." Something in me wanted to divulge ev-erything I had ever longed for, yet I held back.

"What is your name, child?" she gently asked.

"Christina Lafage," I answered.

"Well then, Christina Lafage," she said, "let me tell you what you are asking this god of yours." She went on, "You are looking for a way out, you know you were born for a higher purpose yet you know not what it is. You know deep within you something needs to be awakened. You are asking this god of yours for something which he cannot provide. I know you have doubts, Christina. Do not put your destiny in the hands of one who does not hear you, follow your first instinct."

"My first instinct?" I curiously asked.

"To get out," she smiled, "to follow a different path. Don't follow the herd, Christina, you have an inquisitive and intelligent nature that sets you apart from the rest." Astonished, I asked, "Who are you to see so much?" To which she replied, "My name is Madame Duchamp. I was just like you. I tried prayer and fasting but that is not the way." She held out her hand to me and said, "Come with me, child down the left hand path where all your desires will be fulfilled." Whatever was holding me back at that point disappeared and I felt a strange freedom I had never before felt as I took her hand. I suddenly recognized a kinship with this woman and wanted to learn all she was willing to teach me. "Tell me, Madame Duchamp, isn't the left hand path the way of evil?" I curiously asked.

"Evil," she answered, "is a god who does nothing to answer his followers' prayers. I can give you the world, Christina, but only if you have no fear and renounce this god who does not hear you. I can show you the way of the sorceress if you are willing to learn."

I was intrigued by Madame Duchamp's offer, after all, what good is a god who does nothing to ease the suffering of his people? Leaving with Madame Duchamp would certainly give me the freedom that I longed for and the opportunity to learn the practice of the occult captured my curiosity. My parents had always told me that sorcery was an evil thing but they had also told me that the churchyard that had given me hours of serenity and a safe haven was evil. And yet, I felt no threat or evil intent from this sorceress who stood before me offering me an apprenticeship. But did I have the courage to do it, to reject everything I had been conditioned to believe?

"Life is too short, Christina," she said, sensing my apprehension, "don't drag your feet when you could be running ahead of the pack."

"You present a very enticing offer, Madame Duchamp," I replied cautiously, "but why have you chosen me?"

"I know potential when I see it," she smiled, "you have a fiery passion smoldering deep within you that can do wonders for you with the right guidance."

"But I have no powers," I confessed.

"That will come," she softly replied, "the important thing is the desire and the dedication."

I silently weighed my options. I could stay in the village wasting away and dreaming of a better life, or I could go with Madame Duchamp and actually experience something extraordinary, something I could not get from pious prayer and I realized that she was right. As I rose to my feet I confidently stated, "Madame Duchamp, I am ready to walk the left hand path and I regret every moment I have ever spent in prayer."

"Very well," she said with a smile, "meet me here in this grove at midnight and your journey shall begin."

I walked home elated as if I had just been given all the answers to the universe itself. I was consumed by my newfound freedom while thoughts of wealth and the power of the black arts swam through my mind. With the power of sorcery, I could finally be independent and want for nothing, but I was still under my parents' roof and would have to wait until they were asleep to meet Madame Duchamp in the grove. I knew they would never approve of my accepting such an offer, but I could not turn it down. Fortune had smiled upon me and I would take the chance that had been given to me.

I returned to the village, anxious to be free of the place where I had grown up but never quite felt at home. As I walked to the small house that I shared with my parents, I was full of anxiety and disgust and as we sat down to our meager dinner I pretended to bow my head in prayer but inside I laughed mockingly. My father uttered the blessing over the food and I felt a smile growing across my face and a chuckle erupted from my throat that grew into laughter. My father abruptly stopped and sternly asked, "What in this holy prayer causes you to laugh so?"

"I laugh because you offer thanks to one who does not deserve to be thanked." Horrified, my father stood up and I felt the swift sting of his open palm across my left cheek. But even that could not wipe the smile from my lips. "Are you so blind, father, that you cannot see the truth?"

"All I see," he growled, "is a devilish child before me who appreciates nothing. How can you say such a thing, Christina? Have you not just come from praying in the grove?"

"I have!" I angrily answered, "I have prayed and it has brought me nothing! I have wasted my time praying to one who does not listen!" As I argued with my father, I realized that I was doing just that . . . arguing. I had never raised my voice, let alone *argued* with my father, but I had such a build-up of anger and disappointment that I just let it flow forth in a river of rage and resentment. He was appalled by my defiance and outspoken manner, something I had never before displayed. No longer did I tremble with fear at my father's anger and disapproval. Now that I had a way out, I felt strong and confident. Even as he raised his hand to strike me again, I didn't shrink away with fright; instead I stood firm and coldly stared into his contemptuous eyes.

"Another slap across the face will do you no good," he announced as he slowly lowered his hand, "you need something that will save your soul, Christina. Tomorrow morning I will escort you to the convent, maybe there the mother superior will teach you to have respect for your father and restore your faith."

"That which was never there cannot be restored," I defiantly smiled.

"Go to your bed now and pray for forgiveness for the blasphemy you have brought to this table, for tomorrow begins a cloistered and repentant life for you."

Still wearing my defiant smile, I slowly rose from the table and glanced at my mother who had remained silent and made no attempt to protect her only child. I knew my father's threats would never be carried out; I would be long gone by the time the sun's rays shone on the horizon. I walked proudly to the small bedroom like a king who had just won in battle and lay down on the bed patiently waiting for my parents to retire to their own bed. When all was quiet and close to midnight, I packed up what little belongings I had and started quietly for the front door. Suddenly, I felt a hand firmly grip my wrist, a candle flickered and I saw my father's angry face.

"What business have you outside in the dead of night?" he demanded, "have you been to the churchyard again, against my wishes?"

I felt a confidence and self-assuredness wash over me as I replied, "I have an appointment with Madame Duchamp, a traveler I met this morning in the grove."

"Madame Duchamp!" he interrupted, "That woman is no traveler but a minion of the devil! Has she bewitched you, Christina? Is that where this defiance and blasphemy comes from?"

"How do you know Madame Duchamp?" I asked surprised.

"She was condemned by our village many years ago for heresy and blasphemous acts but escaped before the hangman's noose found her neck," he explained. "Those in her circle were found guilty, tortured and hanged for heresy."

"I have not been bewitched; I go to Madame Duchamp of my own free will!" I exclaimed triumphantly.

My mother had now emerged from the bedroom and begged, "Christina, do not go with Madame Duchamp, if you do, you condemn your soul to eternal damnation."

"If I am to be damned, it is my choice to be so." With that I broke free of my father's grasp and ran out the door and into the night. His footsteps pounded behind me as I ran toward the grove. I was grateful for the moonlight that illuminated the way for me and I could see a carriage up ahead beside the grove – it must be Madame Duchamp! As I ran toward her, I could feel myself being pulled by something unseen toward my waiting benefactor. I finally made it to the carriage and turned to see my father still following in hot pursuit. Madame Duchamp turned toward him, uttered something in Latin and raised her arm to which he abruptly stopped as if frozen, but he could still speak, "Let my child go free, evil devil's whore!"

"I am not holding this girl against her will. She has made her own choice. Christina, do you wish to return to the village with your father or follow your chosen path?" I looked at her and then at my careworn father. "Do what you will, child," she said, "I'll not force you do to anything against your will."

"Madame Duchamp, I come to you of my own free will, but do no harm to my father."

"The girl has made her choice," she said, "Now trouble us no more and you will regain power over your legs at dawn's first light."

I climbed into the carriage with Madame Duchamp as she signaled the driver to go. I looked at my father as he tearfully shouted, "Christina, we will pray for you; we will pray the angels have mercy on your soul!"

"Do not be troubled," Madame Duchamp assured, "No harm will befall your father."

"Thank you, Madame," I quietly replied.

"Is something on your mind, Christina? Do you regret your choice?"

"No, I don't regret my choice," I assured her, "but my father said you were to be hanged for heresy in our village, why did you come back? Weren't you afraid for your life?"

A warm smile came across her smooth, pale face as she said, "Certain herbs that I require grow in that grove where I found you. As for those fools in the village, I have nothing to fear from them. When you have learned all I have to teach you, there will be no one you will fear either."

Her words reassured me and I asked, "Where does my journey begin?"

"Your journey has already begun," she said. "But sleep now, for we will be in my home in Paris by morning."

Paris! At last! A city full of excitement, grandeur and wealthy aristocrats. "Madame, do you think I will find a wealthy nobleman to marry?"

"Marriage," she laughed, "what need have you of a husband when you can have riches of your own? You can have any man you desire for a lover but your wealth will be your own."

"Well, Madame, it seems I have so much to learn. I thought I knew the workings of the world but there seems to be much more," I said wearily.

"Christina, there is a whole other world out there and soon you will learn ways to shape and bend it to your every whim," she assured, "but rest now, for you will need all your strength."

I sank into the soft leather of the carriage and dreamed of Paris as I let the gentle rocking of the carriage lull me into slumber.

2

I awoke in a soft bed covered with linen and smooth silk in a very large finely furnished room. I got out of bed and pushed open the heavy oak door to find Madame Duchamp, when I was startled by a servant. "Where is Madame Duchamp?" I quietly asked.

"Madame Duchamp is with Lady Tiana. I will inform her of your awakening and she will be in to see you."

"Thank you," I replied and returned to the room from whence I had emerged. I walked over to the window and pulled aside the heavy drapes to allow more light to enter when I noticed a long marble table filled with books. My curiosity aroused, I walked over to the table, sat in the comfortably padded chair and began pouring over the volumes of what was sure to be my education. There were books of spells, herbs, divination, necromancy, potions, charms and a book on how to conduct a black mass. It was this volume that caught my eye. I ran my finger over the cool black leather cover and smooth gold lettering before opening and absorbing all the knowledge from its creamy white pages. I learned that the altar is to be the naked body of a young girl and the communion is to be made of blood and flour. The blood is to come from the throat of an unbaptised child and shared by all the participants. I perceived the experience to be decadently fascinating and extremely erotic. I was so engrossed in reading that I did not even hear Madame Duchamp enter the room. "Ah, it seems I have a most anxious student," she proclaimed.

"Oh, Madame Duchamp, I was just reading about the black mass," I said enthusiastically.

"Oh, and what was it that drew you to that particular book?" she sounded pleased.

"It sounds very . . . sensual," I offered. "I had always been told to deny those feelings, as they were evil, but the temptation felt so natural and desirable," I answered and then asked excitedly, "Will we be holding a black mass?"

"In time, Christina, you must be patient. But tell me, are you unknown to man?"

"Yes," I said quietly, "but I do not wish to remain so, I no longer see the reason for virtue."

"Leave everything to me, Christina," she said reassuringly.

"Can you promise me one thing?" I asked.

"Of course, child," she smiled.

"When the time comes," I stated, "I want to be the altar." The smile across her face grew wider and she said, "That pleases me very much, now I know for certain I have made the right choice and you are more than ready to learn the black arts."

Madame Duchamp had led me to the kitchen where I was given a very satisfying meal by her servant, Babette, whom I had met that morning. "Don't eat so much, Christina, do save some of your appetite for this evening," Madame Duchamp gently scolded.

"This evening?" I asked.

"Yes, this evening we begin with your initiation. There will be a banquet following your introduction to the guests and then of course the ceremony," she answered.

"Ceremony?" I nervously asked.

"Have no fear, Christina, I will be with you throughout the evening," she assured.

"Oh, but Madame, I have nothing to wear for such an event," I alarmingly said.

"Not to worry," she smiled, "if you go to the closet in your room your only problem will be which gown to wear." Upon hearing that, I ran from the kitchen back to the room where I had awakened. I rushed to the closet, threw open the door and was astonished to find every color and style of apparel imaginable. Madame Duchamp entered the room and said, "They are all yours, Christina. If you are to be a worldly woman of wealth, you need to look the part."

"They are all so lovely, Madame, but how did you know? Not just about the gowns, but about everything?" I inquired.

"After tonight's ceremony you will know. Now, we must find something for you to wear tonight."

We decided on a black silken gown with a small crystal pendant suspended by a black silk ribbon. "I think this will look simply elegant," smiled Madame Duchamp.

I nervously agreed and asked, "What am I to expect of this ceremony, I feel so nervous."

"I will prepare an elixir to calm you," she said. "The ceremony consists of renouncing your inherited faith and pledging allegiance to the left hand path. I will be with you, so you need not be so nervous. Now, I must go to make sure everything is at the ready for this evening. You should be ready by eight o'clock, Babette will come for you."

Her words reassured me and I began to look forward to the evening's festivities. I decided to rest before the evening's adventure and asked Babette to wake me an hour before I was to make my appearance. I laid down on the bed and drifted into a deep dreamless sleep.

A knocking at the door roused me; time had gone so quickly! Babette entered with a silver goblet and said, "Time has come, Christina. You have one hour to bathe and dress; I will help you with anything you require." My eyes fell to the goblet in her hand. "Oh," she replied, "Madame Duchamp mixed this for you, it calms the nerves." I took the goblet from her and slowly sipped. It had a mildly sweet flavor and a very pleasing smell. I drained the goblet and stepped into the bath that Babette had drawn for me. After being bathed, dressed and perfumed I looked at myself in the mirror. Tendrils of my dark brown hair fell seductively onto my shoulders as Babette painted my lips a deep red. Babette stepped back and said, "Now turn toward me."

I faced her and exclaimed, "Babette you are quite the beautician!"

"You look splendid, Christina, you will do fine. Now let us go." She led me out of the room and down the hallway toward the ballroom. As we drew closer to the huge double doors, I could hear the chattering of the guests above a finely tuned orchestra. I thought by now my heart would be pounding inside my chest, but whatever Madame Duchamp had concocted for me seemed to be working. Suddenly the orchestra stopped and Babette pulled open the doors to the ballroom. Madame Duchamp was standing at the entrance as she took my hand and gave me a comforting smile. The exquisitely dressed guests all had their eyes fixed on me but I strangely felt at ease. At last! I was with the aristocracy where I had always felt I belonged. Madame Duchamp led me in as Babette closed the doors. She then announced, "My dear guests, it gives me great pleasure to present my protégé, Christina Lafage." I gave the guests a slight curtsy that met with warm applause as the orchestra resumed playing. "Christina, you look so beautiful. Come, I will take you around now to meet the guests. You must remember to remain confident but do not appear arrogant. Aristocrats simply hate anyone more arrogant than themselves," she smiled.

The first guest I met was Lady Tiana, the woman Madame Duchamp met with earlier. She was accompanied by Paul LeGrande, who looked much younger than she. When we had taken our leave of the couple, Madame Duchamp told me, "She came to me months ago to create a love potion to give to Monsieur LeGrande. Lady Tiana prefers her lovers very young and very rich. Today I gave her an elixir to restore strength and vitality, he must be wearing her out," she laughed. "So you see," she continued, "there is much wealth to be gained in potions and spells and the aristocracy will be your best customers."

I met various potential customers from the French aristocracy. Everyone was a potential customer to Madame Duchamp.

"The best way to establish yourself," she said, "is word of mouth, especially among the rich."

"Have you created potions for all of these people?" I asked.

"Not all of them," she replied, "some of them have required other services, and some I have not yet worked for."

The last guest I met was the most intriguing one. He was tall and very handsome with raven-black hair neatly pulled back exposing his exquisite features. Madame Duchamp introduced us, "Christina, this is Lucien, he will be presiding over this evening's ceremony."

"I am pleased to make your acquaintance," he said, kissing my hand.

"As am I," I replied. I felt my heart begin to beat a little faster as I looked into his dark eyes and I could swear I detected a slight crimson inside those dark pools.

Just then dinner was announced and all the guests were to go into the dining hall just across from the ballroom. "Do you mind if I sit next to you at dinner?" he asked offering his arm.

"I would be delighted," I said taking his offering.

We walked into the banquet hall and I was amazed at the spread I saw before me. I had never seen so much food; there was everything imaginable to delight the palate of every guest. The table was set with roasted pheasant, quail, platters of beef, a roasted suckling pig, sauces, vegetables, fruits and goblets of wine. I sat between Madame Duchamp and Lucien but my attention was focused mostly on the latter.

He spoke in a deep, soft tone, "So, are you looking forward to your initiation into the black arts?"

"Very much so," I replied.

"Christina will make an excellent sorceress," interrupted Madame Duchamp.

"And a very beautiful one," added Lucien.

"Your compliments are as charming as your name, Monsieur Lucien," I said.

"I have many names," he seductively smiled.

The dinner conversation flowed for hours as the guests discussed fine wine, politics and courtly gossip. I felt someone touch my shoulder and then heard Madame Duchamp whisper in my ear, "Christina, it is time." She then stood up and said, "My dear guests, if you would now return to the ballroom the ceremony will begin. Not you, Christina, stay behind with me while the guests file into the ballroom. You will walk in when you are called forth." I smiled nervously and she said, "Don't worry, I will be right behind you."

The guests were assembled in the ballroom and Lucien called out, "Christina Lafage, come forward!" I took a deep breath and entered the ballroom with Madame Duchamp behind me as she promised. Lucien was standing on the platform where the orchestra had been, holding a rolled parchment.

"When you get in front of him, kneel," she whispered. The guests were on either side of the ballroom as I walked proudly down the middle and knelt before Lucien and marveled at my reflection in his shiny black boots.

"Who brings this girl before me as an initiate?" he demanded.

"I, Madame Madeline Duchamp, sponsor this girl."

"Rise, Christina," he said as he touched my forehead and I felt a jolt of energy rush through me, heightening my senses and leaving me breathless. "Do you come before these witnesses of your own free will and do you deny the guardians assigned to you at baptism and accept Madame Duchamp as your guardian and mentor?"

"I do," I sternly replied, catching my breath.

"Then deny your Christian God by trampling on this," he said as he threw a wooden cross to the floor. I did as he commanded and while still standing on the cross he unrolled the parchment and handed it to me. "You must read this aloud before these witnesses and then sign it in your own blood."

I took the parchment and read, "I, Christina Lafage, hereby promise to you my lord and master my eternal soul and my solemn allegiance. I renounce the Church, God, and Jesus Christ, all the saints, my baptism and all the sacraments. I promise to celebrate an annual black mass in your honor to which a sacrifice of an unbaptised child will be performed. I also promise to pass on all of my knowledge to whomever wishes to learn to follow the left hand path. In exchange, I ask to gain all knowledge and power of the black arts and bend the laws of nature and the spirit world to do my bidding. I ask this in the name of the Lord of the Underworld and seal this pact with my own blood." Madame Duchamp then took my left hand, pricked my thumb with a small pin and held it over a small cup. After a sufficient amount of blood was in the cup, she handed me a pen to dip in the blood and sign the parchment.

"After you sign the pact, give him your necklace," she whispered, "he must have some material possession of yours." I signed the pact and unhooked the clasp that held the crystal pendant around my neck.

I handed the necklace and the unholy pact to Lucien who took them and said, "Welcome to the fold, Christina." His smile reassured me and I knew that I had done well.

"Congratulations, Christina, you have made me proud," proclaimed Madame Duchamp handing me a goblet of wine, "now enjoy the rest of the evening for tomorrow we begin to awaken you to the powers of the invisible world."

The orchestra had resumed playing as Lucien asked, "May I have this dance, Mademoiselle Lafage?"

"Of course," I replied, taking his hand. We danced together most of the evening and I could feel his eyes moving all over me – much to my delight. I was trying to devise a plan to spend some time alone with Lucien so we could become more . . . acquainted. I thought quickly and said, "Monsieur Lucien, you are a marvelous dancer, but I think I need a rest."

"Very well," he replied. He led me across the ballroom to a door that led to a smaller room. "We could rest in here for a while," he smiled seductively.

I could see Madame Duchamp out of the corner of my eye and she nodded with approval. We entered the small room and Lucien closed the door behind us and sat down on the sofa. "Come, sit beside me," he beckoned. I sat down beside him never taking my eyes from him. There was a plate of plump strawberries on a small round table beside him that I had not before noticed. Taking one between his fingers, he said, "These are very sweet," and touched the tip of the strawberry against my lips. My lips parted slightly to allow my tongue to caress the surface of the fruit all the while staring into his dark eyes. I closed my eyes and bit down on the strawberry as he pulled the other half through my lips and into his own mouth. My heartbeat quickened and I felt as though fire was consuming my entire being; if I was to lose my virtue, I surely wanted Lucien to take it. He leaned in and I could feel his hot breath as he pressed his wine-flavored lips against mine. My desire heightened, I opened my mouth to feel his tongue caress my own as he moved his hands over my breasts. I slowly tilted my head back as he planted supple kisses on my neck. I ran my hands over his chest, unbuttoning his shirt, letting it flutter to the floor. By this time he had my dress unfastened and I wriggled out of it with ease lying back on the sofa gently pulling Lucien toward me. "I love a woman who knows what she wants," he whispered.

"I want you, Lucien. Take from me what I've given to no other," I hotly replied. He parted my thighs with one hand while sliding down his trousers with the other. He entered me slowly with the movement of his hips creating a sensual rhythm. I felt as though he would rip me in two but despite the pain I grabbed him, pushing him in deeper. He started to move faster and my pain gave way to unbridled pleasure as I arched my back and reveled in blissful climax. Lucien's breathing became heavier and faster and when he reached his climax I felt an ice-cold substance shoot up inside me. At that moment I knew who Lucien really was and that I had just given myself to the ultimate evil. But it came as no great surprise; I knew there was something about Lucien – something enticingly evil that drew me to him like a moth to a flame.

As he withdrew, we shared a long, deep kiss and then he said, "For someone who has never loved before you are very passionate."

"My lust for you has made me so," I replied.

"I am pleased," he said. "Are you rested enough now, Mademoiselle Lafage?" he coyly asked donning his shirt.

"Well rested and extremely satisfied," I answered, slipping back into my dress.

"Well, then, we should be getting back to the party," he said sliding his arm around my waist.

Some of the guests had left but the orchestra played on before the few couples that remained. "It seems we missed the departure of some of the guests," I said with a sly wink.

"It was worth a night's pleasure," Lucien replied.

We walked over toward Madame Duchamp who had a puzzled look on her face. "Whatever is the matter, Madame?" I inquired.

"I'm afraid some of the guests have had too much wine and linger too long. The hour is late and the orchestra is all but worn out," she laughed.

"Allow me, Madame," offered Lucien. He walked over to the front of the orchestra and announced, "My fellow guests, we have all enjoyed the warm hospitality of Madame Duchamp but the evening has come to an end. Let us all bid adieu to one another and retire for the evening to face another day."

With that, the guests applauded and began to say their farewells to Madame Duchamp. After the last guest had departed, she turned to Lucien and said, "Thank you, Lucien, I can always count on you."

"My pleasure, Madame," he said and then taking my hand, spoke, "I have enjoyed the pleasure of your company this evening, Christina."

"And I, yours," I said as he left a soft kiss on my hand.

I watched as he walked out the door and into the night, part of me wanted to go with him but I hesitated because I knew I would see him again. Madame Duchamp's voice broke into my thoughts, "It will be dawn in a few hours, Christina. You must be tired after your liaison with Lucien," she said with a smile.

"It was very . . . passionate," I replied.

"Ah, yes," she answered, "I remember my first time with Lucien. I was about your age when I was recruited into the black arts and gave myself to Lucien."

"You were recruited in the same manner I was?" I asked.

"Of course," she answered, "just as you will take on a protégé when the time comes."

"When will I know?" I asked.

"You will know when the time comes. You will feel it as absolute confidence in yourself. Now, let us retire for you have much to learn tomorrow."

I bade Madame Duchamp good night and wearily trotted off to my room. I undressed and slipped in between the cool sheets and didn't realize how tired I really was until I laid down and felt every muscle relax. Slumber came almost immediately with dreams of the incredible evening I had just experienced and the new life that lay ahead of me.

The next day found me feeling refreshed and well rested. I dressed and walked to the kitchen to find Babette and Madame Duchamp seated at the small table. "Christina," Madame Duchamp chirped, "I'm so glad you decided to join the waking world. Come, join us. Have something to eat before we begin your training."

I ate quickly, as I was anxious to learn all I could from Madame Duchamp. We rose from the table and Babette pushed it aside as Madame Duchamp picked up the rug to reveal a small trap door. "First lesson – always conceal your workshop," she said, lifting the trap door.

We descended the roughly hewn stairs into a sort of sub cellar. Madame Duchamp picked up a torch and with a wave of her hand a magnificent flame arose illuminating a room full of shelves with various herbs, potions and powders. "Herbs are very important. You should know which ones will induce love, impotency, death, sickness and madness. You need to know not only their names but the proper amount needed for whatever potion you are concocting. See here, I have made up a chart for you; it would be wise to memorize it."

The chart had all the herbs listed, what they were used for and the best time to pick them. "The simplest and most common potion you will be asked to provide is the love potion. The simplest potion for a love spell is to take vervain root, elecampane and mistletoe berries and grind the ingredients to a powder. Add nine drops of your client's blood and have the client add the potion to the wine the desired one will drink."

"And the blood is to come from the left hand?" I asked.

"You learn fast, Christina," she smiled. "Another potent love spell," she went on, "is to carve a waxen image anointed with your client's blood, fasten a lock of the desired one's hair to it and melt the image over a fire. As the wax melts, so will the heart of the one desired."

And so Madame Duchamp went on to teach and I to learn. I learned everything from causing impotence to causing pain and disease to an entire village. Suddenly, there came a knocking from above. Madame Duchamp said, "I will return in a moment. Stay here and study your herbs."

She returned a few moments later and said, "Christina, I want you to come upstairs with me." I followed her up the steps and into the kitchen. I could see the soft purple of twilight out of the kitchen window telling me how long we had been in the cellar.

"Christina, Babette has informed me that Madame Lasalle is here and requires my services. I want you to come with me and observe."

I followed Madame Duchamp into the parlor where her guest was waiting. "Madame Duchamp," she said rising.

"Madame Lasalle, I would like you to meet my protégé, Christina Lafage," said Madame Duchamp.

"It is a pleasure to meet you, Mademoiselle Lafage," she said.

"Likewise," I replied.

"I am very sorry to have missed your gathering last night, Madame Duchamp, but my brother had taken ill," she explained, "He passed away early this morning."

"I am very sorry to hear that, our condolences are with you," said Madame Duchamp, glancing at me. "How can I be of service to you?"

"Well, Madame," she started, "my brother died a very wealthy man; however, he had all of his money hidden somewhere in his house. We have searched the entire house and we have come up empty handed. We need the money for his burial expenses, of course."

"Of course," echoed Madame Duchamp with a hint of sarcasm.

"Madame Duchamp, I need you to . . . speak to him, ask him where his money is," she said. "Of course a sizable portion of the money we find will go toward your fee."

"My fee is required whether or not your brother divulges the location of the money," she politely stated.

"I understand, Madame," replied Madame Lasalle.

"Now," Madame Duchamp said, "when is your brother to be buried?"

"He is to be interred tomorrow morning," answered Madame Lasalle.

"Meet us at midnight in the cemetery on the ninth day after burial," instructed Madame Duchamp, "and tell no one."

"Thank you, Madame," Madame Lasalle graciously replied.

"My servant Babette will see you out, Madame Lasalle, and remember tell no one," she reaffirmed.

When Madame Lasalle had left, I curiously asked, "Can you really raise the dead?"

"We shall see," she smiled. "Now come, we must prepare."

For nine days we prepared. Madame Duchamp explained, "In order to converse with the dead, we must take on the attributes of the dead." We ate only unleavened bread and food with no salt; salt is a preservative and has no place in the grave. The house was kept dark and incense was burning constantly while we were in deep meditation. We could attend no parties or drink wine and by the ninth day, I felt I was one with the despair of the grave.

Madame Duchamp took a red velvet bag and filled it with incense, herbs, candles and a human skull. She threw the bag over her shoulder and handed me a thick book, as we set out for the cemetery in the pale moonlight.

"That book you carry, Christina, is the Grand Grimoire. You will use that book for every incantation or invocation you will perform," she instructed.

Madame Lasalle was waiting at the cemetery gates with an unkempt, rough-looking man by her side.

"Madame Duchamp, this is Louis. He will help us down in the vault," said Madame Lasalle nervously.

"I instructed you to tell no one," Madame Duchamp scolded.

"But Madame, Louis is the caretaker. He has agreed to help us and will be well paid for his silence," Madame Lasalle replied.

"Very well," said Madame Duchamp, "lead us to the crypt."

We walked through the cemetery by candlelight, as torches would have shed too much light on our secret. I felt a sense of excitement as we made our somber trek through the cemetery, past ancient crumbling stones and freshly dug graves. I wasn't exactly sure what would take place, but curiosity was burning inside me. We reached the crypt and Louis pulled open the stone door. A strong odor erupted from the crypt and almost knocked me off my feet. Madame Duchamp caught me by the arm and said, "The smell of death is never pleasant, Christina." I regained my balance as we descended the stone steps into an underground chamber with alcoves built into the walls, some housing coffins and some vacant. There was a damp chill about the place amid the smell of moss-covered stones and death.

I placed the Grand Grimoire on a small shelf as Madame Duchamp handed me the red velvet bag. "Christina, what herbs will we require for raising the dead?" she asked.

"Henbane, hemlock and opium," I confidently replied.

"Very good, you have been studying. You will find those herbs in that bag, place them in this small dish and burn them," she said, handing me the dish.

I did as she instructed and watched the smoke rise and curl up into the darkness. The smell from the herbs soon filled the crypt but still could not overpower the smell of decaying flesh. Madame Duchamp took the velvet bag and removed the skull and a large black candle. She placed the skull in an empty alcove with the black candle burning before it. She then took a small fallen branch and made a large circle-within-a-circle in the dirt floor of the crypt so that there was a small border between the circles. In this border she inscribed the names of demons whose names I found in the Grand Grimoire.

"Louis, can you remove the body from the coffin and make sure the head points toward the east and then wait outside if you please?" asked Madame Duchamp.

"You will find my brother's coffin in the bottom alcove, Louis," said Madame Lasalle who had remained silent but alert to our every move.

Louis had opened the coffin and placed the body on the dirt floor with its head pointing east. "When do I get paid?" he gruffly asked Madame Lasalle.

"When we are through," she replied.

Louis went to wait outside as Madame Duchamp put the bottle of wine in the corpse's left hand. "You see, Christina," she said, "the wine is meant as an offering and the head must point toward the east."

"Why toward the east?" I asked.

"The east is associated with the rising of the sun, so the head must point in that direction in order to rise," she explained.

The corpse lay half decayed in the dirt of the crypt. The eyes were opened in an upward gaze and the mouth had fallen open as if singing a blasphemous hymn. A rat scurried across its blackened, bloated belly as I wondered if it would tell Madame Lasalle what she wanted to know.

Madame Duchamp took a small dagger and proceeded to drag the blade across her left hand, letting the blood rise to the surface and drip into the corpse's mouth.

"The life-force of the blood will cause the corpse to rise," she instructed.

She then instructed Madame Lasalle and myself to step inside the circle. When we were all in the circle, she opened the <u>Grand Grimoire</u> and read, "Hear me, o spirits of the underworld, accept this offering of wine, incense and my own blood and bring forth the spirit of Henri Lasalle."

Suddenly the crypt felt colder and I heard a low moan. "I command you to rise!" said Madame Duchamp, staring at the corpse. "Rise and look upon the living who summoned you!" she commanded.

Slowly the corpse began to stir. To my surprise, it sat up, took a deep breath and then rising to its feet said in a raspy voice, "Why have you summoned me back into this decaying shell?"

"Your sister wishes to ask something of you," replied Madame Duchamp. Madame Lasalle turned pale and looked paralyzed with fear.

"Ask your question," muttered the corpse.

"Henri, is that really you?" she nervously asked.

"Do you not recognize your own brother after he has been lying dead for nine days?" the corpse taunted.

"Henri, I miss you so much but I need to know where you have hidden your money. We still need to pay for your interment," Madame Lasalle said with a quivering voice.

The corpse let out a low, raspy laugh and said, "So, you miss your dear brother? The only thing you miss is your brother's wealth."

"Henri, how can you say that?" Madame Lasalle asked with tears streaming down her face.

"I know that you and that man you plan to marry were devising a plot to get your hands on my money, so I hid it. Look anywhere you please, but you will never find it," stated the corpse.

"Henri, you are my brother, I love you and I would never plot against you," cried Madame Lasalle.

"Love?" said the corpse mockingly, "Did you love me enough to poison me?"

I looked at Madame Duchamp in shock and she motioned to me to stay quiet.

"How could you know that?" Madame Lasalle gasped.

"The dead know many things, dear sister, and I know you will never find my money," replied the corpse.

Madame Lasalle's tears quickly turned to rage as she shouted, "You bastard! You are as miserable in death as you were in life. I pray you never find peace. And as for your money, I will tear your house apart stone by stone until I find it!"

With that, the corpse snarled and lunged toward Madame Lasalle but as soon as it had reached the circle a surge of energy hurled it backwards and slammed it against the wall of the crypt. "I demand that you release my spirit!" it cried.

"Very well," said Madame Duchamp, "go then, and I give you my solemn promise never to summon you again."

The corpse gasped its last breath and crumpled lifeless to the floor. I stood still in the circle, amazed by what I had just witnessed.

Madame Duchamp really had raised the dead! She touched my shoulder and said, "You can come out of the circle now, it is safe."

Madame Lasalle remained in the circle dazed by what she had experienced, so that she did not hear Madame Duchamp call to her. "Madame Lasalle," she repeated.

She slowly turned to Madame Duchamp and asked, "How did he *know*?"

"The dead are privy to even the most secret knowledge," answered Madame Duchamp, "You can call Louis in to put the coffin back into place."

Madame Lasalle slowly walked over to the door of the crypt and called Louis. When he entered, she said, "We are through now, if you would place the corpse into the coffin, I will pay you."

Louis did as she asked and said to her, "I know not what went on in here and I do not care to know. If you will pay me now, I would like to leave this place."

"Did you see what transpired here, Louis?" asked Madame Duchamp.

"I am not sure what I saw but I mean to keep it to myself."

"You would be wise to do so," she replied.

Madame Lasalle handed him a small purse of coins and he quickly left. Madame Duchamp erased the circle she had drawn in the dirt and packed up the skull and the black candle. Turning to Madame Lasalle she said, "Now there is the matter of my fee."

"But Madame Duchamp, my brother refused to tell me where he has hidden his money, you heard him yourself," she protested.

"I told you when you came to me my fee was not negotiable. It would not be wise to cross me," she coldly stated.

"No, it would not be wise to cross you, Madame Duchamp," she said handing her the requested fee.

I was still in awe of what I had just witnessed as we walked home and I noticed how calm Madame Duchamp had been through the whole affair, so I asked her how she was able to do so.

"Christina," she replied, "you must not show any emotion, especially fear. When conjuring the dead or conferring with the spirits you must be the master and show no sign of weakness. If you have fear in your heart, they will sense it and you will have no power over them."

"What about the circle?" I asked.

"The circle can protect you and whoever else is in it, but fear will weaken its protective powers," she replied.

"What will become of Madame Lasalle?" I asked.

"Oh, I wouldn't worry about Madame Lasalle," she said, "her greed knows no end. I really do believe she will tear her brother's house apart to find his money. I'm surprised she waited this long to kill him."

"Madame, may I ask how much you charged her for this evening's work?" I inquired.

"Raising the dead is a very costly affair. All of the preparation, materials and time must be factored into the cost as well as reputation. Since my reputation is well known among the elite and wealthy, they will pay any price I ask. As for Madame Lasalle, her purse is one hundred livres lighter, but I'm sure her wealthy lover will see her through," she laughed.

"One hundred livres?" I gasped.

"Don't worry, you will get your share," she laughed.

The next day started early as we prepared to go down into Madame Duchamp's "workshop."

"Light a torch, Christina," she commanded. I grabbed a torch and started to walk over to the blazing hearth to light it when Madame Duchamp stepped in front of me and scolded, "Not that way." Remembering how she had lit the torch with a simple wave of her hand, I decided to try it. I delicately waved my hand before it, but the torch remained unlit. "You are not focusing your energy. It will take more than a dainty wave of the hand to bring forth fire, now concentrate. You want that torch to be lit, so *see* it lit," she stressed.

I tried once again to light the torch but to no avail. "Maybe I should have left you in bed today," said Madame Duchamp folding her arms across her chest, "now light the damned torch!"

She had never before raised her voice to me and I felt anger starting to rise in me as I shot a quick glance at the torch in my hand. Just then a huge fireball erupted from the torch and blazed upwards, scorching the ceiling. Madame Duchamp quickly raised her hand and as she lowered it so the flame on the torch diminished to a moderate glow.

"Christina, you will control your emotions or you will kill us all," she scolded.

"I'm sorry, Madame, but you have never spoken to me in that manner before," I apologetically replied.

"So I have to invoke your anger to get you to unlock your Power," she smiled.

"Oh, no, Madame, it will not happen again," I assured.

"If you cannot control your emotions, you cannot control your Power," she instructed.

We descended into the cellar and closed the trap door behind us. We walked over to the table and Madame Duchamp pointed to a bottle of sage leaves on the shelf. "Bring that bottle to the table," she requested. I started to walk over toward the shelf when I remembered that conventional ways no longer applied. I took a deep breath and concentrated on moving the small bottle. Tiny beads of sweat appeared on my forehead as I thought of nothing else except moving the bottle. The bottle began to shake and then hurled itself off of the shelf and flew straight toward me. I ducked just in time as the bottle hit the wall and shattered into tiny glass fragments on the stone floor.

"Christina, your Power is strong, you do not need to concentrate so hard," said Madame Duchamp.

"Well, how hard should I concentrate?" I asked.

"When you feel the Power working within you, take control of it. The more you use your Power, the easier it will be to harness it," she replied.

We remained in the cellar most of the day as I learned to "harness the Power" as Madame Duchamp referred to it and pretty soon I could move the bottles without having them crash and shatter and cause the flame on the torch to rise and fall at my command.

"Be patient with the Power and do not get anxious. Patience is the key to controlling the Power," Madame Duchamp instructed.

I was eager to learn and paid close attention to everything Madame Duchamp told me. It was a lot to absorb but I was intent on pleasing my instructor and developing my Power. Most of the lessons came quite easily to me while others required more concentration, but Madame Duchamp was very patient with me; in fact, she had more patience with me than I had with myself. I hated making mistakes, it made me feel inadequate and unworthy of such power, but Madame Duchamp would reassure me and offer compliments contrary to my perception of my abilities.

"Don't be so hard on yourself. You learn so quickly, Christina. I am amazed by your progress," she complimented.

"Thank you, Madame," I replied. I did not think that I had been progressing in great strides but Madame Duchamp seemed impressed. "I guess it is easy to learn something when you have an interest in it."

"Well said, my young protégé," she smiled. "Now let us go upstairs," she said, "I have a surprise for you."

We climbed the steps and emerged into the kitchen as the late afternoon sun beamed through the window.

"Babette, tonight we dine early and I need you to summon a carriage to pick up myself and Mademoiselle Lafage at seven o'clock," instructed Madame Duchamp.

"As you wish, Madame," Babette replied.

"Where are we off to this evening?" I asked.

"Have you ever been to the opera, Christina?" she asked.

"No, Madame, I have not," I answered excitedly.

"Then this evening should be quite an experience for you," she replied.

The carriage arrived promptly at seven o'clock led by a team of magnificent stallions. The carriage itself was smooth ebony with gold trim and lined with deep red velvet. As we traveled down the crowded streets, I was fascinated by all the activity and crowds of people. I really hadn't seen much of the city since my arrival as my studies with Madame Duchamp occupied most of my time. I peered out of the window at the jugglers, musicians and merchants selling everything from bread to brooms. A trained monkey on a long golden leash performed tricks before an amused crowd who proceeded to reward him with coins. A rowdy crowd stumbled out of a saloon, spilled into the street and was nearly run down by our carriage.

Our driver and the crowd exchanged obscenities as we continued on to the opera.

"Paris is such a colorful city, there are so many things going on at once," I said excitedly.

"I am glad you are enjoying your stay in Paris," replied Madame Duchamp, "you've been doing very well and deserve a night out."

The carriage stopped in front of the opera house just long enough for the driver to open the door of the carriage and escort us out. We walked through the huge doors and into the lobby where elegantly dressed aristocrats nodded as we walked by. We were taken by an attendant to Madame Duchamp's private box on the fourth level, stage left. I let my eyes wander to the boxes below that were starting to fill up then to the pit in front of the stage where the orchestra was fine tuning its instruments and finally to the immense stage.

"Well, what do you think?" asked Madame Duchamp.

"Beautiful," I replied, not knowing how else to describe it. The private boxes were intricately carved and draped with velvet with columns dividing them. Those who were not fortunate enough to have a private box were seated behind the orchestra pit in neat rows. Over the stage hung a long black curtain with gold trim running along the top and sides.

The orchestra began to play as a hush fell over the audience. The black curtain then parted to reveal an ancient Roman scene. Here at the opera it seemed that the ancient gods of the past had a home. I watched intensely and marveled at the costumes and scenery on the stage. It was a classic mythological tale of good versus evil with evil being vanquished at the end, but highly entertaining. So much so, that the cast received a standing ovation at the end.

"What did you think of your first opera, Christina?" asked Madame Duchamp.

"I enjoyed it very much; the costumes, the scenery and the music fit together so perfectly," I replied.

"Come now, let us go and mingle in the lobby," she said as she grabbed my hand, leading me out of the box and down the stairs to the marble floor of the lobby.

"Madame Duchamp!" I heard a man's voice exclaim. "Madame Duchamp, it is so good to see you again!" the man said walking toward us.

"Sir James Ridgewood!" she said surprised, "How long have you been in Paris and why have you not come to call?"

"I have been here only a week with my young nephew, but I planned on paying you a visit," he answered.

"I would like you to meet my protégé, Christina Lafage. Christina, this is Sir James Ridgewood of London," she said.

"Charmed," he said as he kissed my hand.

"As am I," I responded.

"Let me introduce you to my nephew, Richard. Richard, where have you gone?" he called.

A tall blond man made his way to where we were standing and politely said, "Here I am, Uncle. Won't you introduce me to these lovely ladies?"

"With pleasure," Sir James replied. "Madame Duchamp, Mademoiselle Lafage, my nephew, Richard."

"It is a pleasure to make your acquaintance ladies," he smoothly replied.

"Madame Duchamp, I am having a party at my hotel this evening. I would be honored if you and Mademoiselle Lafage would attend," Sir James offered.

Madame Duchamp shot me a quick glance and I nodded in approval. "We would be delighted," she replied.

"Very good," he happily stated, "we will take my carriage."

On the way to Sir James' hotel, I learned that he was the leader of the London Hellfire Club, an underground organization of practitioners of the black arts. They held meetings in an abandoned church just outside of London. Madame Duchamp had met him while traveling in England and he had made her an honorary member.

"Madame Duchamp, now that we are away from the crowd and in the confines of this carriage, I would like to employ your services for a most dastardly deed," Sir James said with a smile.

"You have but to ask, old friend," she said. "Well," he started, "there is a certain young lady back in London that I have become very well acquainted with. I have even made her a member of our club; however, we cannot be together as often as we like, you see she is married, so we can only see each other when her husband is away," he explained.

"And what does this husband do?" asked Madame Duchamp.

"He is a general in the army, so he is hardly ever home and the poor girl gets so lonely," he stated.

"And you are the perfect cure for her loneliness, I assume?" she asked with a smile.

"But of course," he replied, "she needs someone who is not away from home so much to satisfy her every need."

"And you are willing to oblige her," she stated.

"You know me so well, Madame Duchamp," he smiled. "So you see, he is a problem and I need your services to . . . remove the problem, shall we say?"

"Come to me tomorrow evening and we shall solve your problem, Sir James," Madame Duchamp said with a wink.

Throughout their conversation, I had exchanged glances and smiles with Sir James' nephew, Richard. He looked to be about my age and very attractive with pale blue eyes and a handsome face.

The carriage had finally stopped in front of the hotel where a crowd of people were waiting. We had all emerged from the carriage as someone from the crowd yelled, "Sir James, where have you been? We've been waiting an eternity!"

"I hardly think I've kept you waiting that long," Sir James laughed.

We filed inside the hotel with the crowd of people, mostly people I had seen at my initiation and some from the opera. Madame Duchamp pulled me aside, handed me a small vial and said, "Drink this elixir, it prevents pregnancy."

"But Madame," I stuttered.

"I saw the way you and young Richard were looking at each other," she smiled, "just in case, better safe than sorry, no?"

I took the vial from her and smiled back, "Just in case."

"Enjoy life, Christina," she said, "for there is no pleasure in the grave."

Sir James had reserved an entire floor of rooms in the hotel for himself, his nephew and any of his friends who wished to stay the night. There were double doors that separated the rooms but they had all been opened so the party guests were free to roam from room to room to discuss the news of the day or play games such as chess or dominoes. Pastries from the kitchen had been brought up to what Sir James had dubbed "the sweet room" and elegantly arranged on a long table.

I was admiring the display when Richard approached me and said, "There is an exciting display of fireworks over the river. I would be honored if you would join me on the balcony to view it, Mademoiselle Lafage,"

"I would be delighted, but please call me Christina," I replied.

We adjourned to the balcony where the heavens had become illuminated with colorful displays. Richard had told me of his travels with his uncle throughout England, Scotland and presently France.

"You have an exciting life, Richard," I said as explosions of light shook the sky.

"And what of your life, Christina? Surely it must be exciting to learn the black arts," he said with a definite interest.

"I have learned and seen things that I dare not speak of, but they have intrigued me and encouraged me to learn more. Are you on the left hand path, Richard?" I asked.

"My uncle's talents are mediocre at best. He was never a serious student. He was always given to fine wine and parties with beautiful women," he admitted. "But Madame Duchamp's talents are well known across the channel and beyond, it must be quite an honor to be her student," he added.

I felt a sense of pride within me as I answered, "Madame Duchamp is a most patient teacher and has the utmost confidence in me. I just hope I don't disappoint her."

"I don't think you are capable of disappointing anyone," Richard said with a smile. "It is obvious she thinks very highly of you," he said moving closer, "you should have more confidence in your talents."

"Some of my talents I am most confident," I said softly.

"I have always believed one's talents are best utilized when they are shared," he said stroking my cheek.

"Seduction seems to be one of your talents, my friend," I whispered.

"That is a talent we both share," he said and then pulled me toward him, kissing me passionately.

"Is there somewhere private we can go?" I asked.

"Come with me," he said taking my hand, "I have a private room."

We walked out of the room with the balcony and down a long hall to the room at the end. Richard had taken a key from his pocket and unlocked the door to reveal a well-furnished suite. I entered the room first, taking the vial that Madame Duchamp had given me and quickly drank its contents before Richard had even entered the room and closed the door.

"Is this private enough?" he smiled, wrapping his arms around my waist.

"It's perfect," I answered before kissing his warm lips.

I wondered how Richard would compare to Lucien as a lover since I had never been with a mortal. We undressed each other slowly savoring every touch and drinking in every kiss. I felt very confident with Richard and he proved to be a very experienced lover with an almost insatiable lust to match my own. He was a passionate and satisfying lover that left me close to exhaustion when we were through.

We lay next to each other for a long time before I heard a knock at the door and a voice softly call, "Christina?"

"Yes, Madame," I answered dazed, reaching for my clothes.

"Where are you going?" Richard asked sleepily.

"Rest, Mon Aimee, I will be right back," I whispered.

I opened the door and could hear the party still going on as Madame Duchamp whispered, "We will be leaving shortly, Christina. I will meet you in the lobby."

"I will be there as soon as I say goodnight to Richard," I said. She nodded with a wink and started down the hallway. I walked over to the bed, leaned over and whispered to Richard, "I must go now."

"Will I see you later?" he asked.

"Of course," I replied, giving him a long, deep kiss.

"Wait, I will see you to the lobby," he said dressing quickly.

3

The next day began late as I joined Madame Duchamp in the kitchen after a long refreshing sleep. "Come, Christina, we must go down to the cellar to prepare for this evening," Madame Duchamp beckoned.

I was about to push the table aside when she stopped me and said, "Get used to using your Power. Now, move the table." I took a deep breath and concentrated solely on moving the table. "Focus all your energy toward the table," Madame Duchamp whispered. Suddenly the table began to shake, but even though I was filled with excitement I remained calm. Slowly, I raised my hands pushing them forward as the table slid smoothly across the floor. Madame Duchamp beamed with price as she exclaimed, "Congratulations, Christina, you have harnessed the Power."

The trap door opened at my command as Madame Duchamp lit a torch and we descended into the cellar. She began lighting incense that quickly perfumed the room. She then went to a cabinet in the corner of the room, removed a large crystal ball and placed it on a wooden base on the long table.

"The incense will set the mood and purify the room," she explained.

"And the crystal ball?" I asked.

"We will be able to see the effectiveness of the spell by gazing into it," she answered. She then brought out two large cushions and placed them

on the floor. "To prepare for a spell such as this, it is necessary to meditate and clear the mind," she instructed. We sat cross-legged facing each
other as she continued, "Now close your eyes, breathe deep and exhale
slowly. Breathe in the perfume of the incense, concentrate on nothing
else but the scent of the air."

I did as she instructed, breathing in the sweet smell of the incense and
exhaling slowly. I began to feel somewhat light-headed, but I kept the steady
rhythm of breathing and concentration. I soon felt as if I was floating up
into the air, becoming one with the smoke from the incense, rising and
curling, leaving my body far below. I was one with the air, light and su-
pernal as if in another dimension. I felt as if I had transcended the physical and became part of the spirit world. Temperature and time no longer
mattered; I felt neither heat nor cold, just an ethereal sense of being with
no concept of time. Millions of specks of light danced around me, floating
and twisting through the air with me. The sensation of not being attached
to my body was exhilarating and I wanted to continue, but I felt something
pulling me back. My eyes slowly opened to see Madame Duchamp standing
over me with her hand on my shoulder with Sir James and Richard standing beside her.

"She is still in the trance?" I heard Sir James ask Madame Duchamp.

"Yes, I do not want to fully wake her. She must be in the trance to see
into the crystal," she whispered.

How long I had lingered in this state I did not know. It could have
been minutes, hours, or days. I rose and let Madame Duchamp escort
me to the table where the crystal ball stood. I felt functional and somewhat coherent yet I lingered in a dream - like state.

Sir James and Richard now joined Madame Duchamp and I at the
long table. Madame Duchamp still seemed to be in a bit of a trance-like
state but was more alert than I.

Sir James placed a sack stained with blood on the table and said to
Madame Duchamp, "The heart of a murderer, just as you requested. He
was executed this morning."

"Excellent," she replied producing a cloth that seemed to have something wrapped in it. She unrolled the cloth to reveal three long, sharp

needles that gleamed in the candlelight. She then removed the heart from the sack and placed it next to the needles.

"Have you something personal from your rival?" she asked Sir James.

"Will a lock of his hair do?" he asked, handing her a small envelope.

"It will do very well," she answered opening the envelope and binding the hair to the heart with a black thread. "What is the name of this rival?" she asked.

"His name is Lawrence," Sir James replied.

"Christina, keep your eyes fixed on that crystal with intense concentration," she instructed.

I did as she requested, but all I saw was my own reflection in the smooth crystal.

Madame Duchamp took a deep breath and began to chant,

"Hear me, demons of the nether regions,

Rise up and gather your legions,

Fly far, across the sea,

Where an evil deed waits for thee."

"May the hair to this heart bound,

Cause this victim to be found

By the spirits who in darkness lurk,

Command this evil spell to work."

As she finished the second verse, my reflection began to fade from the crystal, first becoming cloudy and then clearing to reveal a bearded man standing in front of a table strewn with maps. Madame Duchamp then took one of the needles from the table, raised it over her head, and continued,

"May this first needle make Lawrence weak

And take away his power to speak

So no living soul hears his cries

Or beholds the pain written in his eyes"

She then very forcefully brought the needle down, piercing the left side of the heart that lay on the table. The man in the crystal suddenly fell to his knees and grabbed his throat as if trying to scream. A look of panic swept over his face as he tried to crawl toward the door leading out of the room. Madame Duchamp picked up another needle and continued,

"And may this needle so named number two,

Cause Lawrence pain through and through."

She then stabbed the lower right side of the heart as the man began to writhe in agony on the stone floor of his map room. She went on, picking up the third needle,

"And let the third needle plunge into this heart,

Be the last and command the soul to depart."

The third needle was then thrust into the middle of the heart and the man lay lifeless on the floor with a hideous expression on his upturned face. Madame Duchamp walked toward me, gazed into the crystal and looking up at Sir James announced, "The deed is done."

At that point I didn't know if I was overcome by the sweet smell of incense, the trance I was in or the fact that I had just witnessed a murder, but I suddenly became dizzy and crumpled to the floor. I awoke upstairs in the parlor lying on the sofa with Madame Duchamp kneeling beside me dabbing my forehead with a damp cloth. "Wha-what happened," I asked dazed.

"You gave us quite a scare, child," said Madame Duchamp, "I thought I had lost you."

"The man I saw in the crystal . . ." I said, trying to sit up, "is he . . ."

"Dead of an apparent heart ailment," she finished with a wink. "But rest for a while, Christina, and please accept my sincerest apology."

"Apology?" I said, confused.

"Reading the crystal absorbs a great deal of your energy; I am afraid I did not quite prepare you and for that I take the blame," she said, wiping a tear from her eye.

Richard knelt down beside her and brushed his soft lips against my forehead. "You should rest now as Madame Duchamp suggests," he advised, "may I call on you tomorrow to see how you are feeling?"

"Of course, Richard, you are always welcome here," I answered.

"Well, Madame Duchamp," said Sir James, "I would like to thank you for your services and render the proper payment."

"There is no charge for you, old friend," she said warmly.

"We will see ourselves out and let Mademoiselle Lafage rest," Sir James gallantly stated.

As they left, I let slumber overtake me and drifted into a deep sleep.

Twilight faded into darkness as I stood in an open field that hosted an abandoned stone building that looked centuries old. As I moved closer, I could make out the tall steeple of an ivy-covered church pointing at the darkened sky as moonlight shone on the adjacent graveyard. A faint mist gathered and hovered around the crumbling tombstones, then seemed to rise and fade into dancing spirits. I could almost hear the music that enchanted them and I longed to join their dance. I started toward them swaying to their ghostly rhythm, when I beheld something out of the corner of my eye. A dark figure stood in the doorway of the church beckoning me. I heard it softly call to me with a voice as gentle as a lover's caress. My attention shifted from the cemetery ghost-dancers to the solemn figure in the doorway. I could not see its face, yet it seemed familiar to me. Ever closer I drew toward it and I felt its touch on my shoulder as I heard it whisper, "Soon."

My eyes shot open to see Madame Duchamp above me gently shaking my shoulder. "Soon what?" I asked.

"Whatever do you mean, Christina?" she asked perplexed. She knelt down and I proceeded to tell her about the dream and the dark figure in the doorway of the church.

"Sometimes our dreams are foreshadowings of things to come or things that we desire," she explained.

"It was so real, I could swear I heard it whisper to me," I said.

"I have no doubt it whispered to you in the land of dreams, but do not struggle with its meaning in the waking world. If something is to be revealed to you it will come when the time is right," said Madame emphatically.

We were both startled by a loud knock at the front door. Madame Duchamp rose as I heard Babette open the door.

"I need to see Madame Duchamp right away!" a man's voice blurted forcefully.

"It is a bit early for visitors, monsieur," I heard Babette tell the nameless stranger.

"Wait here, Christina," instructed Madame Duchamp. She left the parlor closing the door behind her. I quietly rose from the sofa and crept over to the door, slightly opening it to hear the early morning commotion.

"You don't understand!" I heard the stranger exclaim, "I must see Madame Duchamp!"

"But monsieur," I heard Babette say before Madame Duchamp broke in, "I am Madame Duchamp and who are you to come here at this early hour and accost my servant?"

"My sincerest apologies, ladies, my name is Andre LeBlanc. I have come to employ your services."

"We do not accept clients at this hour of the morning, Monsieur LeBlanc, please come back this afternoon and then we will see if we can help you," replied Madame Duchamp.

"As you wish," he sounded disgusted, "I will return this afternoon."

"I am sorry, Madame, I did not wish for you to be disturbed," Babette apologized.

"It's all right, Babette," Madame Duchamp assured, "it seems Monsieur LeBlanc needs to learn some manners."

I quietly closed the door and hurried back to the sofa just before Madame Duchamp entered the parlor.

"We will have a client this afternoon, Christina, I'm sure you heard," she smiled.

"Yes, I heard," I answered feeling my face begin to blush and then remembering how Monsieur LeBlanc had acted, asked, "We will still work with him even though he was so rude?"

"Never turn away a paying customer, Christina," she replied. "Remember, we have the Power, therefore, we always have the upper hand. Besides, you need the experience."

The hour was early but I was wide awake and did not bother with trying to go back to sleep, so I went into the kitchen with Madame Duchamp for an early breakfast. I kept thinking about last night's events, particularly about the man I saw in the crystal. Was he really dead? Had I indeed been witness to a murder?

"Is something on your mind, Christina?" Madame Duchamp asked, "You've been very quiet."

"I was just thinking about last night," I confessed, "did that man I saw in the crystal really die by your hand?"

"Well, not *directly* by my hand," she smiled mischievously, "but it was by my command."

"But Madame," I whispered, leaning across the table, "you committed a murder, does it not *bother* you?"

"When you perform spells such as the death spell, you must not let emotions or morality interfere," she explained. "I did not know that man. Therefore, I felt no remorse for taking his life. It was just a favor to Sir James."

"I don't know if I could ever perform a death spell, Madame," I said quietly.

"That takes time, Christina. You first must be able to detach your-self from emotion. As you grow older and wiser and come to understand the workings of the world it will be easier for you to make that decision. It didn't come easy for me either when I was your age, but remember, I am always here for you," she assured squeezing my hand. "Now if you will excuse me, I would like to have a long, hot bath before Monsieur LeBlanc returns this afternoon."

As she left the kitchen I poured another cup of coffee and walked outside into the chilly autumn morning. I thought about what Madame Duchamp had told me and why I felt so uneasy about last night's events. Was I really uneasy about the death spell, or was there still a frightened child lingering deep with-in me? I had the power to move objects, light torches and certainly to kill, but would fear stop me? Surely it had not stopped Madame Duchamp and she had always told me not to have any fear, but could I really kill without remorse?

The sun began to warm the morning air that rustled through the red and orange leaves on the trees as I contemplated what I was afraid of. I sat outside for some time feeling the warm sun on my shoulders, as my coffee grew cold. I heard the shuffle of footsteps behind me and turned to find Babette coming toward me.

"Madame wishes for you to come inside to prepare for Monsieur LeBlanc," she stated.

"Very well," I sighed and followed her into the house.

I soaked in a warm herbal bath for a good half hour. The warmth of the water and the smell of the herbs soothed me and helped to put my mind at ease.

I met Madame Duchamp in the parlor where she had just lit a cone of sweet-smelling incense.

"Ah, Christina, are you feeling better?" she asked.

"I feel quite relaxed," I replied.

"But still a bit uneasy," she finished.

"Well, yes," I answered. "I still do not understand how you can kill without fear of consequences."

"Consequences," she laughed, "Who would catch me? The man you observed in the crystal died alone. There was no one to blame nor any evidence of foul play. We are all killers, Christina. Whether we choose to admit or ignore it is another matter. But trouble yourself no further, the death spell is not required; however, it is very profitable. There will come a time when you will be ready and you will have no fear."

There was a soft knock at the parlor door as Babette announced that Monsieur LeBlanc had arrived.

"Show him in, Babette," Madame Duchamp replied.

Moments later Monsieur LeBlanc had entered the parlor. He was an older man in his fifties, I would guess, rather plain looking and of short stature.

"Madame Duchamp, my deepest apologies for this morning. I have been quite agitated since my mother's passing a fortnight ago. It was very sudden and quite a shock."

"My deepest sympathy," replied Madame Duchamp. "Allow me to present my protégée, Christina Lafage."

"Charmed, Mademoiselle Lafage," he said as he kissed my hand with the look of a hungry wolf in his eyes.

"It is a pleasure to make your acquaintance," I said cautiously.

"What can we do for you, Monsieur LeBlanc?" Madame Duchamp asked as I took note of her usual friendly but businesslike manner which she would perpetuate through the whole conversation. Madame Duchamp had a way of getting her clients to open up to her as if they were confiding in an old friend, but I knew she cared little, if any, about their problems. To her it was all part of negotiating the deal; to me it had become an admirable quality, one that I had yet to master and surely would under Madame's tutelage; but for now it was time to observe and listen as Monsieur LeBlanc explained his need for our services.

"As I have stated, my mother passed away and she was interred wearing her favorite ring, a gift to her from my late father before they were married. I have recently heard disturbing rumors regarding Marcel, the undertaker. It has been said that he steals from the dead before he buries them. At first I regarded this as just idle gossip, but when I attended a party last night and saw the undertaker's daughter wearing the same ring that was supposedly buried with my dear mother, I was barely able to contain my anger and shock over the very idea that someone could stoop to such a level."

He spoke with such dramatic flair that it would have made any stage actor envious. I would have thought him more sincere if he didn't keep shooting lustful glances toward me. I found it arousing coming from Lucien or Richard, but from this man it made me feel most uncomfortable.

"That is why I came to see you," he continued. "I want that ring back. Is there any way you can help me?"

"Well," Madame Duchamp stated, "this sounds like something best handled by the authorities. Have you gone to them?"

"I went to them right after the party. They questioned the undertaker and he of course denied everything. He said he bought the ring from some traveling merchant months ago," he contested.

"I see," said Madame pensively, " and you are sure the ring belonged to your mother?"

"Absolutely. My father had it specially made in London," he proudly replied.

"I believe we can help you, Monsieur LeBlanc," she said sympathetically, "it is quite appalling to learn that someone could perform such a vile act as to steal from the dead. Return here tomorrow evening with seventy-five livres and we will prepare for you an amulet to help you recover your stolen property."

"Seventy-five livres?" He questioned, "that is quite a lot of money."

"I am sorry, Monsieur LeBlanc, but our fees are not open to negotiation. When you see the results of the amulet, you will see that it is well worth the price," she assured.

"Very well," he relented, "seventy-five livres it will be."

"If you will excuse us then Monsieur, Christina and I have much work to do," she stated.

"Of course, Madame Duchamp. I will return to you tomorrow evening," he replied as we all rose to our feet. "I look forward to the pleasure of your company, Mademoiselle Lafage," he said to me, again displaying the hungry-wolf look in his eyes.

"Thank you, Monsieur," I said coolly.

As Madame Duchamp escorted him to the front door, I felt a sense of a relief wash over me and I would be glad when our business with him was finished.

Madame Duchamp came back into the parlor with a sly smirk on her face as she announced, "I believe Monsieur LeBlanc was quite taken with you."

"I can assure you the feeling is not mutual," I replied.

"It is wise not to mix business with pleasure; I don't think that will be a problem for you in this case," she laughed.

"Certainly not; by the way, what amulet did you have in mind?" I asked, changing the subject.

"Which amulet would you choose?" she asked, testing me.

Fortunately, I knew the answer and proudly replied, "I would use the Hand of Glory, of course."

"Precisely, but we must wait for nightfall before obtaining such an amulet," she instructed.

I was about to retire to my room for further study on amulets when I heard a carriage outside.

Madame Duchamp knowingly looked at me and said, "I've a feeling you have a guest."

I left her in the parlor and hurried down the hall to the front door. Babette already had the door open and I got there in time to see Richard emerge from the finely gilded carriage.

"Christina," he smiled as I ran toward him, "You look wonderful, much better than last night."

"And you look as handsome as ever," I replied, kissing his soft lips.

We spent the afternoon together walking through the garden, talking and realizing we had similar backgrounds. Richard's parents were farmers from a small village, much like my own. He had never shown any interest in farming, much to his father's dismay. Like myself, he longed for something more than a mundane existence. The only joy he received was when his Uncle James came to visit and would tell Richard of his adventures and distant lands. When Sir James had formed his

Hellfire Club, Richard's parents banned him from their farm and their son, so when Richard came of age, he left for London to join in his uncle's adventures.

Sir James had been involved with a woman of wealth and power who had bequeathed her fortune to him upon her untimely passing. It was never known if Sir James had anything to do with his lover's death, as he had made some powerful friends who saw to it that no charges were ever filed or investigated.

When Richard arrived in London, Sir James was delighted and set up a trust fund for his young nephew who was eager to join his London Hellfire Club. The club's members were all practitioners of the Black Arts, who made potions and held Black Masses, but none were as skilled as Madame Duchamp; according to Richard, Madame Duchamp was "held in the highest regard."

The sky above began to grow dark and a chill returned to the autumn air as I explained to Richard that I had to get back home for the preparation of the Hand of Glory for Monsieur LeBlanc. I told him the entire story of that morning and afternoon and how uneasy I felt around Monsieur LeBlanc.

"It sounds as if this man has more than Madame Duchamp's services in mind," Richard said with a hint of what I suspected to be jealousy.

"Well, I can assure you," I said, sliding my arms around him, "he'll get nothing from me."

He smiled as he pulled me close and kissed me deeply.

"We had best be getting back," I whispered, even though I wanted to stay in his warm embrace.

"Do you think I could accompany you this evening, just to watch?" he asked.

"I would have to ask Madame; she usually prefers that we work alone, but I will speak to her," I said confidently.

We walked home in the fading twilight amidst the acrid smell of burning leaves in the distance. We arrived home and went into the parlor, but Madame Duchamp was not there.

"Wait here," I told Richard, "I know where to find her."

I went into the kitchen and down into the cellar where I was sure to find her.

"Christina," she said, "I was beginning to worry, I thought you had forgotten."

"Oh, no," I assured, "but I do have something to ask of you."

"What can I do for you?" she asked, removing a small hatchet from the wall.

"Would it be possible for Richard to join us? I know that you prefer we work alone, but he really seems interested," I pleaded.

"Interested in the Black Arts or you?" she coyly asked.

"I believe both subjects hold his interest," I answered.

"Very well," she relented, "Richard can come with us, we do need someone to act as a lookout." Her tone then turned serious, "Christina, I know you and Richard are involved with each other, but you realize your training takes precedence, do you not?"

"I will let nothing stand in the way of my chosen path," I assured her.

"Excellent," she replied, "now let us be on our way."

We made our way to the parlor where Richard was waiting.

"Richard, can you act as a lookout for us this evening?" asked Madame Duchamp.

"My services are yours, Madame," he replied, "where are we off to?"

"We go under cover of night to the gallows," she said picking up a small sack.

The three of us left the house and stealthily made our way to the gallows where two criminals had been hanged that evening.

"We are in luck," she whispered, "they have not yet cut the bodies down."

She instructed Richard to wait at the foot of the gallows and warn us of any approaching pedestrian. We carefully climbed the steps of the gallows to where one of the corpses slowly swayed at the end of its rope.

"Take hold of the forearm and middle finger of the left hand and hold tight," she softly instructed as she cut the bound hands apart.

I lifted the dead limb and held it as she instructed raising it to about eye level. Touching the cold, dead flesh made my skin crawl and sent an icy chill down my spine, but I held the limb tightly. Madame Duchamp took the bag and pulled out the small hatchet, which she raised over her head and with one swift blow, severed the hand from the left arm of the hanging corpse. I stood there still holding the middle finger of the hand watching the blood drip onto the dirt below. Madame Duchamp handed me a cloth and instructed me to wrap the hand in it as she pulled a small dagger from her pocket and sliced open the corpse's thigh. She worked quickly, removing the fat from the gaping wound and placing it in a round metal container. She took the hand from me and placed it in the sack along with the metal container and the hatchet.

"Our work here is done," she said, motioning me to descend the steps of the gallows.

As I walked down the thirteen steps I looked for Richard but he was nowhere to be seen. "Richard," I called softly, "where are you?"

"Here, Christina," he finally answered emerging from behind the gallows. "I thought I heard something, but it was only a rat."

"You saw no one?" asked Madame Duchamp who handled descending the steps of the gallows as swiftly as she handled the hatchet.

"Not a soul," replied Richard.

We walked home with our gruesome treasure as thick clouds floated across the moon.

"What is to become of the hand?" Richard asked. He had been shooting quick glances up to the gallows while watching for curious onlookers.

"Now we have to prepare the hand for its use as a talisman," I answered.

Thunder rumbled in the distance as a light rain began to fall. We had just made it home when the rain got heavier and the thunder rumbled closer.

We walked into the house and straight down into the cellar. Madame Duchamp unwrapped the hand and went to squeeze the blood out of it, letting it drip into a glass jar.

"Christina, can you melt some wax in this?" she asked, handing me a small metal pot.

"Yes, Madame," I replied taking the pot and dropping a chunk of wax into it. I took the candle from the shelf but rather than lighting it from the torch, I called upon the Power. I placed the candle on the table and concentrated on a small flame fit for a candle. I envisioned the candle being lit and with a slight motion of my index finger a flame rose and danced on the wick of the candle. Madame Duchamp nodded with approval and I looked over at Richard seated in the corner wide-eyed with amazement. I held the pot over the candle flame and the wax began to melt. When the block of wax was about halfway melted, Madame Duchamp opened the metal container and added the fat that was sliced from the corpse's thigh.

"Let these melt together," she instructed. She then took an earthenware jar partially filled with salt, placed the hand inside and covered it with more salt. "We need to remove all moisture from the hand," she explained, "the salt will dry it out perfectly."

The wax and fat had melted and blended to form a thick liquid that I poured into a candle mold according to Madame Duchamp's instructions.

"There is no more we can do tonight, the rest is for tomorrow," she announced.

We all adjourned to the parlor for tea and to rest from the evening's activities.

"What will you do tomorrow to complete the talisman?" Richard asked.

"Christina," Madame Duchamp said, once again testing me.

"The hand will be removed from the salt and the candle will be inserted into it. It will then be placed in the sun and dried."

"Excellent," she proudly stated. "Now if the two of you will excuse me, I think I will retire for the evening."

"Good night, Madame Duchamp, and thank you for allowing me to accompany you this evening."

"You are quite welcome," she replied. "Not too late, Christina," she winked.

"This evening has proved to be quite an interesting one," Richard said sitting down beside me and finishing his tea.

"Would you like something stronger than tea?" I asked.

"That would be lovely," he answered.

"I'll not be a minute," I said, leaving the parlor and heading for the wine cellar with a quick detour down into the workshop to mix up the contraceptive elixir. Downing the elixir, I quickly returned upstairs to the kitchen with a bottle of our finest vintage. I had just closed the trap door when I thought I glimpsed a figure through the kitchen window. I hurriedly threw open the kitchen door and ran out into the rain to give chase, but the elusive phantom disappeared into the black sheet of the rainy night. The rain soaked my skin as I scanned the yard for any intruder but could discern none. I went back into the kitchen, grabbed the bottle of wine and returned to the parlor.

"Your wine cellar is rather wet," Richard laughed.

"I thought I saw someone outside, but nothing was there except for the rain," I explained.

"Are you sure?" he asked, rising to his feet and joining me at the parlor entrance.

"I am quite sure," I said, uncorking the wine.

"You should get out of these wet clothes," he said, taking my hand, "come over by the fire."

He released me from the bonds of my wet clothing as we lay down before the warm fire blazing in the hearth. He took me into his arms and I kissed him deeply letting my hands unbutton and unfasten until his bare flesh was against my own. I rolled on top of Richard and began to ride him slowly, becoming unequivocally immersed in the steady rhythm. Deeper and faster our rhythm became until we were both writhing with pleasure in the warm firelight. He pulled me close in a tight embrace and whispered, "I love you, Christina."

"I love you, too," I answered, stunned. I did love Richard, but I never thought I would hear those words emerge from his lips.

"You sound surprised," he smiled.

"I've never had anyone say that to me before," I confided, "I didn't think I would hear it from you."

"Why would you think that?" he asked.

"You've experienced so much more than I -- travels with your uncle to distant lands, parties with all sorts of interesting people. My life has been very secluded up until Madame Duchamp took me under her wing," I explained.

"Well, actually, I've never said that to anyone before," he confessed, "I had never felt it until that first night we spent together. Of all the women I have met, none are as beautiful or as intriguing as you."

As much as I loved him, I knew that my training with Madame Duchamp was my priority, so I nervously asked, "Will you stay with me, no matter where my chosen path leads me?"

"Absolutely," he replied, "I would not ask you to abandon that which you were chosen to do."

Outside, the rain came heavier as it danced to its own rhythm on the roof and windowpanes. I had told Richard to stay the night rather than brave the storm trying to get to his hotel. We quietly crept to my room where we fell asleep nestled in each other's arms.

The morning sun beamed through the window as my eyelids slowly opened to greet it. I rose quietly as not to disturb Richard and headed for the kitchen. Using the Power to move the table and open the trap door, I descended the stone steps into the cellar. The earthenware jar that contained the hand still stood on the table where we had left it. I slowly opened it and pulled out the gruesome talisman. The salt had made the hand quite leathery and dark in color, however, it was still not completely dried out. I took it upstairs and placed it outside in a concealed location in the yard where the sun could finish the drying out process.

It was still early, so I crept back to my room to enjoy a few more hours of sleep in Richard's arms.

"Where were you?" he sleepily asked as I entered the bedroom.

"I just had to check on the talisman. I wanted to make sure it is ready when Monsieur LeBlanc arrives. I'm anxious for our business with him to be over," I confessed, sinking into his arms.

"If this man makes you that uncomfortable, I could stay with you when he comes to pick up his talisman," Richard offered.

"No, that is not necessary. I can handle Monsieur LeBlanc," I said confidently.

We slept until late morning, when a frantic knocking at the door awakened us. I opened the door to find Madame Duchamp with a look of concern on her face as she asked, "Christina, where is the talisman?"

"Don't worry, it is safe," I replied as I led her outside to where the hand lay drying in the sun. "I checked it this morning, but it wasn't quite dried out," I explained.

"I'm glad you knew what to do, but next time please let me know when you remove something from the cellar," she said, relieved.

We brought the hand back inside and curled its leathery fingers around the candle we made from wax and the corpse's own fat.

"Now it is ready," said Madame Duchamp, admiring her handiwork.

I wiled away the afternoon with Richard, strolling around the city and having an early dinner at his hotel before returning home to present the Hand of Glory to Monsieur LeBlanc.

"Are you sure you don't want me to stay?" Richard asked.

"I'll be fine," I assured, kissing him goodnight, "I will see you to-morrow night." He left reluctantly as he climbed into his carriage and threw me a kiss.

Madame Duchamp was already in the parlor when I entered. "When is our guest due?" I asked.

"About half an hour," she replied, "how was your afternoon with Richard?"

"We had a lovely afternoon," I beamed.

"Do you love him?" she asked.

"Yes, I do," I happily answered.

"Has he asked you to make a choice between himself and the path you've chosen to follow?" she asked in a very serious tone.

"No, Madame," I answered, "he wants me to stay on the path."

"Really?" she asked surprised, "such a quality is rare in a man."

"Richard knows how important it is to me," I proudly smiled.

"I'm sure he does," she replied, "but remember, love comes and goes, stay true to the path."

I nodded in agreement as there came a soft knock at the door.

"Madame, Monsieur LeBlanc has arrived," Babette announced.

"Very good, Babette, show him in," Madame Duchamp replied.

Monsieur LeBlanc entered the parlor looking a lot calmer than that of his first visit.

"Good evening, ladies," he said smoothly.

"Good evening, Monsieur LeBlanc," said Madame Duchamp. "I know you are most anxious to retrieve your stolen property."

"Indeed I am," he stated sternly.

"Then allow me to present you with The Hand of Glory," she said, unveiling the gruesome talisman.

Monsieur LeBlanc's calm expression turned to one of shock as he asked, "What is that?"

"The Hand of Glory," I repeated, "fashioned from the left hand of a hanged man. Simply place the hand outside the undertaker's house while they are asleep and light the candle. As long as the candle is lit, the inhabitants of the house will not wake. You can enter the house, retrieve your property and leave without anyone knowing you were ever there."

"Well done, Christina," Madame Duchamp whispered.

"And how do I extinguish the flame?" he asked.

"Pour milk over the wick and that will extinguish the flame," answered Madame Duchamp, placing the hand in a sack and handing it to Monsieur LeBlanc.

"Very well," he said, regaining his composure and handing Madame Duchamp the requested price. "Madame Duchamp, I hate to be a bother, but I have a dreadful headache. Could you possibly render some healing potion for me?" he asked, rubbing his right temple.

"It is no trouble, Monsieur LeBlanc, I will be but a moment," she replied as she left the parlor and left me alone with Monsieur LeBlanc.

There was an uncomfortable silence, which he soon broke with, "You are very beautiful, Mademoiselle Lafage," he said as he sat next to me. "I looked forward to seeing you all day. I wonder if we might see each other later this evening. I can promise you a very exciting time," he said leaning toward me and placing his hand on my knee.

I quickly rose and calmly stated, "I am flattered, Monsieur LeBlanc, but I do not mix business with pleasure."

"Ah, but I am not interested in business," he replied.

"I am sorry, Monsieur, but I am already spoken for," I told him.

"I don't mind, that just makes the prize that much sweeter," he said, approaching me, "and you would be such a sweet prize," he whispered as he put his arms around my waist and forcefully pulled me toward him. I broke free of his grasp and let all of the rage and anger I felt toward him explode in one hard, violent slap across his surprised face. "You willful bitch!" he hissed. "You will pay for that!"

"I think not!" I angrily replied as I looked up at the crossed swords that hung over the fireplace. One of them began to twitch and then it flung itself from the wall as I reached up and grabbed the handle.

"Take one step closer and I will slit your miserable throat!" I shouted. Just then, Madame Duchamp burst into the room.

"What is going on in here?" she demanded.

"It seems Monsieur LeBlanc is somewhat overzealous with his passions," I answered, still holding the sword and never taking my eyes from him.

"Forgive me, Madame Duchamp, but I paid Mademoiselle Lafage a compliment which she seems to have taken the wrong way," he lied.

"I would hardly call attempted rape a compliment," I said angrily.

"Monsieur LeBlanc, take your talisman and leave," she said sternly, "and never come here again."

"But Madame," he started, "allow me to . . ."

"Leave now!" she shouted, "Or so help me, I will allow her to kill you!"

He picked up the Hand of Glory and shot a hateful glance in my direction, but I still held onto the sword, unwavering.

"Do not come here again or near Mademoiselle Lafage or myself or we will be your last memory," Madame Duchamp severely stated.

"Madame, is everything all right? I heard shouting," Babette said, entering the parlor.

"Everything is fine, Babette," Madame Duchamp replied, "please show Monsieur LeBlanc out, he will not be returning."

He angrily stormed out as I relaxed my grip on the hilt of the sword. "Christina, I am so sorry, I never should have left you alone with that scum," she apologized.

"No need to worry, Madame," I assured, "I think I really would have killed him."

"And how did that feel?" she asked.

I answered her most honestly when I replied, "It felt . . . exhilarating."

Madame Duchamp had taken the sword from me and returned it to its location over the fireplace. Babette had re-entered the parlor with some tea as I sat and took a deep breath. "So now you are not afraid to kill," Madame Duchamp said, sitting next to me.

"I really would have killed him had you not intervened. I actually *wanted* to kill him, I could taste it," I confessed.

"I have no doubt that you would have," she replied, "you had the cold look of a killer in your eyes."

"But Monsieur LeBlanc was not an innocent victim," I said, remembering the death spell I had witnessed.

"Everyone is guilty of something, Christina," she laughed, "you'll sleep better if you remember that."

We sipped our tea and talked well into the night before Madame Duchamp announced that she was retiring for the evening. Not feeling tired myself, I decided to stay up to read a fascinating book on amulets and talismans. I read through half the book when my eyelids began to get heavy. I put the book aside and walked out of the parlor, when I heard a sound coming from the front door. As I moved closer, I could see someone fumbling with the lock. What thief would attempt to break into this house? I decided I would throw open the door and surprise the would-be robber, but not without being armed. Madame Duchamp always kept a dagger in the drawer of the small table in the hallway, which I quickly removed and quietly reached for the doorknob. My heart was racing and

I could feel beads of sweat on my forehead as I turned the knob and threw open the door. There, with a look of shock on his face, was Monsieur LeBlanc with the Hand of Glory just outside the door blazing forth with its hideous light.

He looked at me and then down at the hand and said nervously, "You told me I could use the hand more than once, that it would work so long as the candle burns!"

Seeing him trying to break into the house and trying to use the talisman that Madame Duchamp and I prepared to exact his revenge on me left me furious and burning with rage.

"You fool!" I shouted, "You cannot use my own talisman against me!"

He lunged toward me pinning me against the wall. The firm grip he had on my wrist forced me to drop the dagger as he tore at my clothes and said, "No one denies me. I always get what I want."

"Not this time you don't!" I replied as I summoned all my strength and pushed him off of me, causing both of us to stumble out the door and down the steps. We stood up facing each other as I quickly looked over at the Hand of Glory that was still ablaze outside the door.

"Now it ends," I said gravely as I directed my concentration toward the hand. The fingers began to uncurl themselves from the candle causing the candle to roll down the steps and into the dirt. A strong wind arose as Monsieur LeBlanc took a step toward me. The wind began to swirl, picking up the hand and hurling it at the throat of Monsieur LeBlanc. A look of horror swept over his face as he struggled with the talisman that gripped his throat. The harder I concentrated, the tighter the hand gripped its victim's throat until he was on the ground gasping for air. I stood over him and watched until his struggling ceased and he gasped no more. A powerful but exhilarating rush of energy shot through me, taking my breath as it made my entire body tingle and my heartbeat quicken.

"Christina!" I heard Madame Duchamp shout over the still swirling wind. I took a deep breath and exhaled slowly as the wind died down to a gentle breeze. Madame Duchamp and Babette ran toward me as I turned to face them.

"Christina, what happened? I heard shouting and when I came out here the wind was blowing so hard, I called to you, but you could not hear me!" Madame Duchamp said frantically.

"He tried to break in," I said breathlessly, looking down at the lifeless body of Monsieur LeBlanc, "he even tried to use the Hand of Glory, but of course it would not work against us."

"And you killed him," Madame Duchamp softly uttered.

"Yes, I killed him," I spoke up, "he deserved it."

"Yes, he did deserve it," she agreed, "I would have done the same."

The three of us dragged the body of Monsieur LeBlanc into the house and down into the cellar.

"I think this will be easier if we put him on the table," Madame suggested. We lifted the body onto the table with the hand still firmly attached to its neck. The eyes bulged out of the face that had now begun to turn a dark shade of purple.

"What do we do now?" I asked.

"We have to dispose of the body," Madame answered, "the easiest way is to dismember it."

"And what about the Hand of Glory?" I asked.

"I recovered the candle from outside," Babette announced.

"Then we will save it," Madame replied as she pried the fingers from the corpse's bruised neck. "Well, let's get started," Madame suggested as she handed me a saw. All three of us worked on dismembering the unwanted intruder that I had unleashed my anger upon. It took us hours to complete the job that left us covered in blood and sweat. The body now lay in pieces on the table; hands, arms, legs, feet and head lay in a gruesome arrangement. Madame Duchamp went over to the far left corner of the cellar and moved a small bookcase that concealed a trap door underneath it. She lifted the trap door and motioned for Babette and me to start bringing over the bloody pieces that used to be Monsieur LeBlanc.

"The acid in this pit will eradicate all traces of Monsieur LeBlanc."

The pit resembled a small but a deep well that could have reached to the very bowels of hell itself. The acid bubbled and churned as we dropped the body parts down into the pit. There was a distinct hissing sound as the acid devoured flesh and bone piece by piece. The head was the last to be lowered into the pit and I stood to watch the acid eat away at the grotesque face until it had melted away.

"Serves you right," I muttered as Madame Duchamp lowered the trap door.

"Are you all right, Christina?" she asked, "you've been through a lot this evening."

"I am fine, Madame, just exhausted," I answered wearily, "but there is one thing."

"Yes?" she said.

"When I killed Monsieur LeBlanc, I felt something," I confessed.

"The Power," she replied, "whenever you take a life, your Power becomes stronger and you feel it. The more lives you take the stronger you will become."

"Right now it has exhausted me," I replied.

"We are all in need of rest," she stated as we climbed the stone steps. I went straight into a hot bath to scrub away the sweat and blood that stained my skin. When I finally got into bed, I could just see the first light of dawn.

Once again I found myself in the churchyard with the dark figure in the doorway of the church. I still could not see its face, but I could hear it whisper to me, "I look forward to seeing you again, Christina."

"But who?" I started to ask before it put an icy finger to my lips.

"You already know," it whispered as it disappeared into the church. I followed it inside but it was nowhere to be found. I was standing at the foot of a long aisle flanked on each side by rows of decaying wooden pews. There was a flicker of light at the end of the aisle near the altar, but I couldn't distinguish what was going on. As I began to move closer, the figure emerged from the shadows barring my way and softly said, "Not now, Christina, soon."

I awoke back in my bed before I had a chance to ask what was soon to be revealed to me. The late afternoon sun flooded the room as I rose and drew back the drapes. Laughter echoed from the parlor and I decided to dress quickly and join in whatever was going on. After last night's events and the recurring dream, I felt I needed a diversion.

I entered the parlor to find Madame Duchamp in the company of Sir James and Richard.

"Christina, I'm glad you joined us," Madame Duchamp smiled, "Sir James and Richard have just arrived."

"With an enticing request," Sir James broke in.

"Anything for you, my friend," she replied.

"In two weeks time," he continued, "we will be returning to England for the annual Black Mass. I would be honored if you and Mademoiselle Lafage would join the London Hellfire Club for this event."

I looked at Madame Duchamp hoping she would accept Sir James' invitation, although I could not see why she wouldn't. She looked back at me and read the excitement on my face and replied, "We would be delighted to be your guests, Sir James."

"Splendid!" Sir James exclaimed.

"Christina has expressed a desire to be the altar," she stated, looking over at me, "that is still your wish, is it not?"

"Absolutely," I replied.

"Excellent," Sir James stated, "Have you ever attended a Black Mass before, my dear?"

"No, Sir James, this will be my first," I said confidently.

"Well, then, it's settled," he affirmed, "I have already chartered a ship to take us to England that will leave two weeks from today."

"You certainly are prepared, Sir James," said Madame Duchamp as Babette entered the parlor with a bottle of champagne. "A toast to Sir James," Madame Duchamp announced pouring champagne for all of us.

"To Sir James," Richard and I echoed, draining our glasses.

"It's a beautiful afternoon, Christina, would you like to go for a walk?" Richard asked.

"I would love to," I replied, "would you excuse us, Madame?"

"Certainly," she smiled.

Richard took my hand and led me out into the cool air of the afternoon. "How did everything go last night?" he anxiously asked. I decided at that moment to be honest with him and not spare any details. I loved him and could not imagine lying to him, so I began to relate all of last night's events. About midway through my account, I could see his face beginning to turn red and he erupted with anger. "I knew I should not have left you, how dare he try to force himself on you! I swear I will kill that bastard!" he roared.

"There is no need, Richard," I said trying to calm him.

"No need?" he angrily questioned.

"It seems I've beaten you to it," I smiled and went to complete my tale.

Richard was intrigued, "Tell me, what was it like to hold someone's life in the palm of your hand and having the power to extinguish it by your own will?"

"It was . . . perverse, but extremely intoxicating," I confessed. "That was the first time I unleashed my full power; it was quite exhilarating."

"And of course revenge is sweet," Richard added.

"Vengeance never tasted so delightful," I agreed.

"I still should not have left you," he repeated, "I feel somewhat responsible."

"There is no need for you to feel responsible, Richard. What happened was no fault of yours," I assured him as he pulled me toward him. "You would have killed for me?" I slyly asked.

"Of course I would have," he responded, caressing my cheek. I leaned in toward him tasting his warm kiss and feeling his quickening heartbeat. I felt my passion awaken as we lay down in the soft grass and made love in the fading sunlight.

The next two weeks kept me very busy preparing for our trip to England. I was packing and studying with Madame Duchamp during the day, preparing potions and casting mild spells for the wealthy and then spending the nights with Richard. The time seemed to go very quickly as the morning of our departure arrived to find us rising early to wait for the carriage that would take us to the dock.

"Have you ever sailed before, Christina?" Madame Duchamp asked.

"No, never," I answered excitedly.

"You had better drink this for nausea," she said, handing me a small vial, "the waters of the English Channel can be quite rough."

I took the vial from her and swallowed its contents just as the carriage pulled up to speed us off to our waiting ship.

Sir James and Richard were waiting at the dock when we arrived. "Good morning, ladies," Sir James chirped, "We will have the porter load your luggage, as we are just about ready to set sail."

"Thank you, Sir James," replied Madame Duchamp, "and what a beautiful morning."

"Beautiful indeed," smiled Richard, greeting me with a kiss.

The vessel that was to carry us across the channel was quite small, but Richard assured me that it was sturdy enough to navigate the choppy waters of the channel. I looked down into the dark water as we boarded the vessel and wondered what secrets it held.

"Are you nervous?" Richard asked, helping me onto the vessel.

"Not at all," I answered, "just excited."

The hours of rough sailing across the channel made me grateful for the potion Madame Duchamp had given me just before we left. "Is it always this rough?" I asked Sir James.

"These are very turbulent waters, my dear, but have no fear; I have crossed these waters many times without incident," he confidently replied.

We reached the shore by late afternoon and were whisked away to Sir James' estate on the outskirts of London.

"Please make yourselves at home, my dear guests," Sir James announced upon our arrival.

Inside the house, I noticed the servants were busying themselves preparing for a large party.

"There will be a banquet later this evening," Sir James explained, "all of the members of the London Hellfire Club will be here and you and Madame Duchamp will be my honored guests."

"I am very much looking forward to it," I replied.

"You should go now and get some rest," he suggested as he instructed a servant to show Madame Duchamp and myself to the guest rooms.

"Until later, my love," said Richard, giving my lips a gentle kiss. I wanted him to join me, but I really did need some rest, as I was sure the party would last well into the evening.

The guest room I was shown to was lavishly decorated with intricately woven tapestries covering the walls and an immense window overlooking an elaborate garden. I didn't realize how tired I was until I laid down on the soft bed and began to doze. Slumber had brought the dream upon me again and I was closer to the hooded figure than I had ever been, but I still could not see its face. Its hand gently closed my eyes as I felt the kiss of its familiar lips. Long and deep was its kiss, lighting the fire of passion deep within me. I wanted it to take me right at that moment and quell my dark desire, but I awoke before I could follow through.

I did feel well rested, despite the dream and got up to prepare for Sir James' soiree. I had just finished getting dressed when I heard a faint murmur of voices then a knock at my door which I promptly opened to find Richard handsomely attired and very alluring.

"May I escort you to the banquet hall, Mademoiselle Lafage?" he asked, offering his arm.

"But of course," I answered.

He took me to an immense room with a ballroom on the right and a huge banquet table on the left that displayed a unique palette of foods. The room itself as well as the atmosphere reminded me of Madame Duchamp's ballroom where I had my initiation so many months ago.

"You look beautiful," Richard whispered and I smiled back at him as Sir James and Madame Duchamp came toward us.

"Richard, do you mind if we steal Mademoiselle Lafage away from you for a while? I would like to introduce her to our guests," Sir James declared.

"Not at all, uncle," he replied.

"I will see you in a little while," I sweetly whispered to him.

"I'll be waiting," he smiled as I turned to go with Sir James and Madame Duchamp.

I was introduced to many members of London society, all of who were members of Sir James' club. Some were members that one would not expect, such as magistrates, judges and even a few from the clergy. Most of them either knew or knew of Madame Duchamp and treated her as well as myself with the utmost respect and courtesy. The last person we met was Sir James' recently widowed mistress, Rebecca. She was young, attractive and according to Sir James, "well worth killing for." They stayed together for the remainder of the evening, arm in arm, talking and laughing with the rest of the guests.

I felt a soft kiss brush the back of my neck and spun around to find Richard's smiling face.

"Come with me," he whispered as he took me by the hand and led me out of the banquet hall and outside into the garden. The chilly autumn air made me shiver, which Richard noticed and draped his coat over my shoulders.

"Where are we going?" I asked.

"For a stroll," he answered, "you have been so busy all evening meeting the guests, I just wanted some time alone with you."

We walked through the garden in the waning moonlight and came upon a huge greenhouse that doubled as an indoor garden. The air felt warmer as we entered and we were greeted by the sweet scent of autumn flowers. We wandered through the pathways of the greenhouse lined with marble statues and fountains surrounded by all sorts of fall foliage and evergreens.

"The Black Mass is tomorrow night," Richard said with a smile, "are you sure you want to go through with it?"

"I am ready and I have been looking forward to it for a long time," I replied.

We sat on a stone bench beneath an ivy-covered gargoyle as a very thin crescent moon peeked through the clouds, barely illuminating the greenhouse.

"Take this and wear it tomorrow," he said removing a small onyx stone from around his neck. "I bought it from an Arab trader. It's always brought me luck. I want you to have it," he said placing the silken cord around my neck.

"Thank you, Richard, I will wear it always," I said with a kiss. "It's beautiful here, Richard," I softly confessed.

"I knew you would like this place," he said, stroking my lips with his fingers as I began to kiss them tenderly, letting my tongue caress them one by one. His hands then gently removed his coat from my shoulders and I laid back on it, pulling him toward me. His kisses came long and deep as he lifted my skirts and I lustfully wrapped my legs around him. I could feel his hot breath on my neck as he slid inside me creating a blissful ecstasy. I held him tight and closed my eyes as we let our bodies relish in a passionate climax amidst the enchanting surroundings of the greenhouse.

The moon had disappeared behind the clouds as we made our way back to the house where the party continued, loud and boisterous. The evening went well and an enjoyable time was had by all the guests. It was near dawn when the last of the guests had departed and we retired to our rooms for a long rest.

I awoke in Richard's arms nestled in the warmth of his body. I felt refreshed since the recurring dream I had been having did not disturb my sleep. I heard the clock chime four times and I tried to wriggle out of Richard's embrace without rousing him, but to no avail.

"No, stay," he sleepily uttered.

"It's late afternoon, I must go prepare for tonight's ceremony," I explained, "I will see you later."

I left a kiss on his forehead and exited the room to find Madame Duchamp coming down the hallway.

"Christina, I was just coming to wake you," she declared, "you must prepare for this evening."

She took me to a dimly lit room where I soaked in a hot bath as Madame Duchamp chanted phrases in Latin and added aromatic herbs and scented oils to the water. Madame's chanting as well as the herbs relaxed me, yet all of my senses felt heightened. I withdrew from the bath and was given a black robe by Madame Duchamp.

"You will wear this tonight for the ceremony," she instructed. Slipping the robe over my head, I took delight in the cool softness against my bare flesh.

"And now clear your mind," she continued, "think of nothing else but tonight. I will be back for you later."

She then lit some mild incense and quietly left the room. I sat on the plush carpet and stared at the two candles that scarcely illuminated the room. I began to notice shadows deep within the candle flames performing some sort of ritualistic dance. They seemed to be dancing in a circle around something that could have been a building or a large altar. They fascinated me as I became entranced by their unbroken rhythm. I could even see myself joining in their dance and losing myself in their world.

I lingered with them for quite some time until I felt a strong presence beside me, not a hostile one, but one strong enough to return me to the darkened room with the flickering candles.

"Christina, the time has come. Rise and walk with us," Madame Duchamp's words came serious but comforting. I felt elated as I rose and turned to face her. She was in a similar black robe and held a blazing torch that illuminated the whole room and the hallway where a procession of black-robed figures bearing torches was waiting. With Madame Duchamp, Sir James and myself heading the procession, we filed outside into the moonless night. We walked until we came upon the now familiar churchyard that had been plaguing my dreams. As we drew closer, I could see a hooded figure retreat into the abandoned church and I tried to quicken my steps, but Madame Duchamp grabbed me by the arm to keep me in line with the rest of the torch-lit procession.

When we had finally made it to the church, Madame Duchamp whispered, "Let everyone else enter, you will be the last."

I nodded as she walked into the church with the rest of the procession. Richard was the last in line and I took him in my arms and whispered, "No matter what happens, I love you."

"I understand," he answered as we parted and he joined the others inside.

I took a deep breath and started down the aisle into the church. The smell of henbane, nightshade and myrtle incense filled my nostrils and I felt as if I was floating. The hooded figure was standing at the end of the aisle behind a stone altar draped with a black cloth, beckoning me closer. I walked past the decaying wooden pews filled with the guests from the previous night's party toward the hooded figure that haunted my dreams. As I approached the altar, the figure drew back its hood and revealed Lucien's finely chiseled features.

"It's a pleasure to see you again, Christina," he said softly.

"I am yours, my Lord," I replied as he removed my robe and motioned for me to lie back on the altar. Two large candlesticks holding tall black candles were then placed in each one of my hands as Lucien performed the sign of the cross backwards and addressed his flock, "Greetings, children of darkness. We gather tonight in this unholy place to worship supreme evil and perform acts that dare not be performed in the light of day."

Sir James, who was in the front row, came up to the altar, knelt down before Lucien and announced, "And we come here to honor you, Master, to offer our thanks for the dark Powers you have bestowed on us."

Just then I heard an infant cry as Sir James' mistress, Rebecca, approached the altar and handed a bundle to Sir James. Sir James, still kneeling, lifted the bundle over his head and declared, "We offer you this unbaptised babe as a sacrifice to your glory, Master, and asked to be baptized in blood."

Lucien placed a silver chalice on my stomach and took the tiny child from Sir James. The cold metal against my bare flesh sent a chill through me, but I did my best not to quiver. Madame Duchamp approached the altar and knelt before Lucien, offering him a long dagger with strange symbols carved into the handle.

"For you, my Lord," she said. He took the dagger, placed it against the crying infant's throat and made a clean cut. I could feel a warm puddle dripping onto my flesh as he held the open throat over the chalice with the red blood streaming and filling it until the lifeless body was drained.

"Behold, the untainted blood of the innocent!" Lucien exclaimed, holding the chalice above his head, "Come forward now and renew your allegiance to the left hand path. Drink from this cup of devotion and be baptized in blood!"

I saw Sir James hand Lucien a plate of communion hosts, which Lucien cursed and spat upon as the congregation, began to approach the altar. One by one they consumed the blasphemous host and drank the slaughtered infant's blood. After the last of the congregation had taken the unholy communion, Lucien placed a host in my mouth and lowered the chalice to my lips.

"Drink, Christina," he bade, "drink deep."

I sat up and drank the still warm liquid from the chalice and lay back on the altar as Lucien leaned over me and licked the blood from my moistened lips. I felt the deep fire of arousal beginning to burn within me with every stroke of his smooth tongue. I looked into his dark eyes as he stood over me and smiled seductively as a member of the congregation approached the altar and knelt before him.

"Master," he spoke, presenting two waxen images, "I have given my wife everything she wanted, and I was a faithful husband and a good provider. But despite my efforts, she has left me for another man and has taken all I have given her – money, food, and luxuries – and now shares them with this man. They have made a mockery of me and I will not be satisfied until both of them lay rotting in the grave. I beseech you to curse these effigies and exact my revenge."

Lucien took the wax figures from him and placed them on my stomach, spat on them and sprinkled them with the remaining blood from the chalice.

"Now stab each figure through the heart and melt them over a small fire; as the wax melts, so will they die a slow agonizing death," he smiled as he handed the cursed figures to his disciple.

"Thank you, my Lord," he replied returning to the congregation.

Lucien then picked up the chalice and sprinkled myself and the rest of his followers with the blood that remained in the silver chalice.

Sir James approached the altar and knelt down before Lucien as he proudly stated, "Master, we thank you for your presence here and everything you have bestowed upon us, we are renewed in your strength."

"Thank you, Sir James," Lucien replied as Sir James kissed Lucien's left hand. "All of you have proved your allegiance to me and now it is time for feast and revelry," Lucien announced as the congregation began filing up to the altar to kiss the left hand of the dark prince before exiting the church.

Lucien closed the door after the last of the congregation had left and headed back toward the altar where I still lay with the blood from the sacrifice beginning to dry on my skin.

"Well, my fair maiden," he said, removing the candlesticks from my hands, "you make a most beautiful altar."

I was hypnotized by his soft voice and especially his dark eyes, much like prey gazing into the eyes of the serpent right before it strikes. He ran his smooth hands over my stomach and the dried blood began to liquefy at his touch, warm and thick as he spread it all over my body. His sensual massage made every part of me ache for him as my breathing became heavier and I began to quiver. Throwing his robe aside, he began caressing me with passionate kisses and licking the blood from my breasts as he lay on top of me. I untied the ribbon that held back his jet-black hair and let his soft mane slowly spill onto my skin as he raised his head and I hungrily kissed his sanguine lips. My eyes closed in ecstasy as he entered me with the motion of his lovemaking smearing both our bodies with the sacrificial blood. My fingernails dug into his back as the passion became more intense and I thought my spine would snap as I arched my back in tempestuous climax. Beads of sweat ran down Lucien's face as the rush of his cold seed made me shiver.

His hot passion faded into a sardonic smile as he withdrew declaring, "You've done well this evening, Christina."

"Anything to please you, my Lord," I responded as he kissed my forehead.

"My anticipation of this evening has been well rewarded. I'm glad it has been in your thoughts as well as your dreams," he smiled.

"So, it has been you invading my dreams," I gently chided.

"Dreams are just one of the ways I influence mankind . . . and woman," he confessed, "I can reveal what will come to pass, what has been or uncover your deepest desire."

"So were this evening's events what you were trying to show me?" I asked.

"On the first night we met, you knew you would see me again, so your dream wasn't entirely my doing, but I did look forward to seeing you again," he smiled.

"Do you mean in exchange for the Power you have given me, you can read my thoughts?" I asked.

"I know everyone's thoughts, my lady, from the purest virgin to the most vile criminal. I know that you have used the power to kill . . . and have enjoyed it," he confessed.

"But that was self-defense," I protested.

"Come now, Christina, do you deny the exhilarating rush of Power you felt as you took Monsieur LeBlanc's life?" he knowingly asked.

"I should know better than to hide anything from you. I cannot deny what I felt, I did enjoy it *immensely*," I confessed.

"Never deny your feelings, Christina, it will only make you weak. Find strength in your desires and revel in who and what you are, walk the path with pride but use the Power wisely. To wield the Power foolishly would be your undoing," he instructed.

"I witnessed Madame Duchamp perform a death spell," I confided, "at the time I wasn't sure if I would be able to take a life, but even though the rush of Power was thrilling when I killed Monsieur LeBlanc, I still don't know if I could kill without probable cause."

"Christina," he smiled, caressing my cheek, "you are so young and life still holds many experiences and lessons for you. You will take many lives before your time on this earth is through, those both just and unjust."

I got up from the bloodstained altar and donned the black robe I had worn when I entered the church as Lucien asked, "And what of this evening's sacrifice? If I had asked you to kill the infant, would you have done it?"

The killing of the infant had not bothered me as much as I thought it would. Maybe it was the intoxicating feeling I had gotten from the incense, or the fact that I had read about the Black Mass and knew what to expect or maybe I was getting used to bloodshed. So I answered Lucien honestly, "Yes, I would have. I know my Lord demands the sacrifice of the innocent and could not have refused. I swore my allegiance to you and would not break my oath."

"Madame Duchamp has taught you well," he smiled. I leaned toward him and he kissed me tenderly. "Now go and join the feasting and revelry outside. You've done very well," he stated proudly.

"Thank you, my Lord," I replied and started down the aisle toward the door.

I wondered when I would see Lucien again and when I turned to ask him, all that remained was the bloodstained altar and the dancing smoke of the incense.

The cool outside air felt refreshing as I pushed open the door of the church and inhaled deeply. As my eyes opened, I saw Richard coming toward me as bonfires blazed in the distance. Seeing Richard made me feel guilty about being with Lucien, even though it was part of the ritual.

"Richard, I . . ." I stammered solemnly.

"I know you have to do what the Master asks of you," he began, putting his finger to my lips, "whatever happened inside should remain between you and Lucien."

I was sure Richard knew what went on after the congregation had left but wanted to be spared the details.

"I love you, Richard," I said falling into his arms.

"I love you, too and always will," he replied.

We shared a kiss as I heard Sir James roar, "Come you two, the celebration awaits!" We followed Sir James, arm in arm into the festive night. The churchyard was ablaze with bonfires as members of the congregation feasted and drank merrily, while many couples reveled in the pleasures of sex. A band of musicians began to assemble with drums, viols and recorders creating a thunderous wall of rhythm providing the perfect accompaniment to the festivities.

Groups of people started toward the church and began dancing around it, circling toward the left, as the music grew louder. I watched them intensely and heard a voice whisper, "Go join them, Christina."

I turned around to find Madame Duchamp behind me with a very distinguished-looking gentleman by her side. "What are they doing?" I asked dreamily.

"They are dancing widdershins," she replied.

"Widdershins?" I asked. "Toward the left," she explained, "join the dance."

"Won't you come with us?" I asked.

"I have another matter to attend to," she replied with a wink.

I took Richard by the hand and we approached the circle of dancers, swaying and skipping to the swelling music. I could actually feel the music inside every fiber of my being as I let the rhythm take me. It was as if I was being pulled by some unseen force and my body was no longer my own, but a slave to the music. Whirling and leaping along with the music put me into such a euphoric state that I came to understand what pure exaltation felt like. When the music had finally slowed and stopped, I was near the brink of exhaustion as Richard pulled me out of the circle and carried me to a grassy spot beneath a gnarled oak.

"Christina, are you all right?" he asked dabbing my forehead with his handkerchief.

"Richard," I whispered, trying to catch my breath, "I'm fine, I just became so overwhelmed. What an experience! Did you feel it, too?"

"I felt a rush of exhilaration, but not as intense as you must have felt," he declared.

I described my euphoric feeling and experience to him as I regained my strength and composure.

"Why don't we get some refreshment?" Richard suggested.

"That's an excellent idea," I agreed.

There was a long table set up in the churchyard filled with bottles of wine and platters of food giving off luscious aromas that made me realize how hungry I really was. We ate, drank, and laughed as the night wore on and for the first time I felt that I had everything I had ever wanted.

"Enjoying your evening?" Madame Duchamp asked as she approached us.

"Very much, Madame," I replied, hugging her.

"Lucien said you were exceptional this evening," she whispered in my ear.

I smiled in response and quickly changed the subject. "Where is your escort?"

"Oh, he's off somewhere, I'm through with him," she winked. "Are you enjoying yourself, Richard?"

"Absolutely, Madame, any time with Christina is enjoyable," he replied kissing me softly.

"Well, then," she said, "I will leave you to enjoy your time together. But remember, we must leave before dawn to avoid discovery."

"No need to worry, Madame," I assured.

Dawn's first light was hours away, so we made our way back to where the food and drink were set up and Richard happily uncorked a bottle of wine. I took the bottle from him and took a hearty swallow before handing it back to him. He smiled as he took me in his arms and kissed me by the blazing bonfire and while locked in a passionate embrace, I thought I heard hoof beats in the distance. As his lips separated from mine, I heard Madame Duchamp and Sir James shouting, "We must leave now!"

"But . . ." was all I managed to get out before Madame Duchamp grabbed my hand and we began to run. Richard was right behind us as we ran past the church and toward the forest. I could hear people screaming and shots being fired, though I did not know why. We stopped behind a cluster of trees and crouched down in the damp grass.

"What's going on?" I asked between heavy breaths.

"It's the town magistrate and his henchmen," Sir James answered, "I don't know how they found us."

"Round up the rest of the heretics and we will take them back to stand trial!" I heard a man's voice command.

"That's William Moorsgate," Madame Duchamp whispered to Sir James.

"You know him?" I asked surprised.

"William Moorsgate, on the church's authority, has been trying to infiltrate and destroy the London Hellfire Club for years, but he could never find out where we held our meetings," Sir James explained.

"We should get out of here," Madame Duchamp suggested.

"Head deeper into the forest," Sir James instructed as we stood and ran for cover in the forest.

"Stop! Stop!" I heard William Moorsgate shout as he and one of his henchmen started after us.

"Run, Christina!" Richard shouted from behind me as shots rang out and I turned to see Richard fall.

"Richard!" I screamed, as Madame Duchamp and Sir James ran back to help me carry Richard into the safety of the forest. We managed to lose our pursuers in the shadows of the tall trees and laid Richard down on a bed of pine branches.

"Richard," I whispered, my eyes welling with tears as the branches became warm and sticky with my lover's blood.

"Christina," he said softly, "it's so cold."

I held him close to me to try and keep him warm as Madame Duchamp tried to stop the bleeding from the bullet wounds that ripped through his body. She looked up at me very sadly and shook her head.

"There must be something you can do, please Madame," I cried.

"Christina, he's lost a lot of blood, there are some things that are beyond even my power," she tearfully stated.

"Christina, it's dangerous here," he gasped, "leave me."

"No!" I cried, "I will not leave you here!"

"If they catch you, they will torture you. I don't want that to happen to you," he said between shallow breaths, "Madame Duchamp has chosen wisely, stay on the path."

"But without you . . ." I wept.

"Let nothing deter you," he interrupted, "the Power serves you well."

He winced in pain as he put his arms around me and whispered, "I love you, Christina," and with one final breath, his body went limp.

"Richard, don't leave me!" I sobbed but to no avail.

"My beloved nephew," Sir James said mournfully, "if I could switch places with you, I would."

I felt as if my heart had been ripped from my chest as I lay sobbing with my fallen lover in my arms.

"Christina," Madame Duchamp said tearfully, "we must go."

"No," I sobbed, "I cannot."

"Christina, I can't leave you here, we must go now!" she insisted. Just then I heard footsteps and the click of a cocked trigger.

"Well, Sir James Ridgewood," William Moorsgate said smugly, "we finally meet."

All of my sadness and grief suddenly turned to red hot anger upon hearing that man's voice and I slowly rose to face him.

"You killed him!" I said angrily through bitter tears.

"I sent his wretched soul to the devil where it belongs," he said looking down at Richard.

" You insolent bastard!" I spat at him as his henchman put his finger on the trigger of the rifle.

"Don't shoot her!" Moorsgate commanded. He took two steps toward me and I felt the back of his hand knock me to the ground. "You have a very sharp tongue, young lass," he said angrily, "nothing that fifty lashes with the whip won't cure."

Madame Duchamp stepped forward and furiously replied, "You won't get away with that, Moorsgate!"

"And you must be Madame Duchamp," he said smoothly, "whose heresy and wicked acts of blasphemy are well known, even across the channel."

"No, Madame," I said as I scrambled to my feet, "this one is mine."

"Do what you will, Christina," she relented.

"Kill them!" Moorsgate barked, but before the henchman could reply, I shot him a quick glance and the rifle he was holding began to glow red with heat causing him to abruptly drop the weapon and grasp his hands in pain.

I could feel the anger growing and burning within me as I began to chant,

"Dark prince, hear my plea,

As blood assured my pact with thee,

Sound the call, toll the bell,

And open wide the gates of Hell!"

Moorsgate's henchman ran off, leaving his master to face his fate alone. "Run, you coward," he scolded, "I don't need you." I started toward him as he attempted to intimidate me, "In the name of the Christian God, I command you to be silent!"

His command made me even angrier as I continued toward him and resumed the chant,

"In the name of evil, do what I ask,

Send your minions to perform this task,

Command them to let havoc wreak,

And unleash the vengeance that I seek!"

Moorsgate read the rage on my face and heard the hate in my voice as he turned and ran like the coward he really was, back toward the cemetery. But I would not back down, I would have my vengeance. I caught up to him in the cemetery where a red mist began to gather as I shouted,

"As I, in my own tears submersed,

Declare that William Moorsgate be cursed,

By all the power of the left hand path,

So you, Moorsgate, will suffer my wrath!"

The cemetery was soon engulfed in the red mist and began to form into hideous beings that stopped Moorsgate in his tracks and began tearing at his flesh with their sharp claws. Moorsgate screamed in terror as the beasts of the mist grabbed his limbs and began flaying the flesh from his writhing body and devouring it with their laughing mouths. I stood defiantly in front of him as he prayed in vain for death to take him.

"Who are you to have such control over these demons?" he asked in between prayers.

"I am Christina Lafage, and I wield more power than you could ever imagine!" I sternly replied.

"You will pay for your evil power and your blasphemy with your very soul!" he rebuked.

"Pay? The only one who will pay is you, with your miserable life!" I angrily snarled as I plunged my fist into the bloody pulp of his torso. He screamed in agony as I exclaimed, "For my Richard!" and wrenched his heart from his once proud chest condemning him.

"Behold the heart of William Moorsgate,

To haunt this land is now his fate,

I command that his torment never cease,

And his wretched spirit never finds peace!"

I threw the still warm heart to the ground and spat on it as the demons of the mist devoured it and the rest of what remained of William
Moorsgate as once again the rush of Power bolted through my body and
made my senses reel. Madame Duchamp took me by the hand as we
walked toward the church where members of our congregation had been
bound in chains. Sir James found keys on one of Moorsgate's henchmen
who had been stabbed in the onslaught and began freeing the prisoners.

Rebecca, who had managed to elude capture, came running over to
Sir James crying, "I was so worried they captured you. Are you all right?"

"I am fine, but Richard has been killed," he morosely explained.

"Oh, I am so sorry. Is there anything I can do?" she asked.

"We need to get Richard's body out of here," he instructed, "where
are the rest of Moorsgate's men?"

"They ran off when they saw the red mist over the cemetery," she
answered.

The members of the London Hellfire Club accompanied us to where
Richard's body lay and carried him back to Sir James' estate. With broken heart I helped Madame Duchamp and Sir James wash Richard's body
and prepare him for burial. Dawn was on the horizon as the members
of the London Hellfire Club assembled in a secluded spot on Sir James'
estate to bid farewell to one of their own. Sir James tearfully read a
passage from the Grand Grimoire that had been Richard's favorite and
I clutched the onyx stone around my neck that he had given me. I was
inconsolable as his body was lowered into the earth. My tears flowed
endlessly as we walked back to the house where Madame Duchamp took
me into her arms and held me as I wept.

"Christina, I know this is difficult for you," she consoled, "and I am
here for you."

"I feel so empty," I sobbed, "how can such happiness be snatched away
so quickly?"

"Life carries no guarantees," she imparted, "even we are not immune to pain and loss. But I know you are strong enough to withstand this."

"I don't know that I will ever get through the pain, I loved him," I cried.

"I know you loved him, Christina, and I wish I could tell you that the pain will go away, but I cannot. In time the pain will diminish but it never goes away, it just becomes easier to face," she said trying to comfort me.

"I can't imagine it getting easier, nor can I imagine life without Richard," I lamented.

"Time heals, Christina," she said, "I know right now your wounds are deep, but you will heal. Now, why don't you get some rest, it's been a long, traumatic night."

"Yes," I replied, "I need to be alone for a while."

I retired to the guest room where I lay for a long time thinking about Richard before crying myself to sleep.

4

 awoke in the late afternoon to the rhythm of the autumn rain pounding against the window. I was hoping that the previous night's horrors had all been a dream, but the empty space next to me in the bed had confirmed the grim reality. My love was gone and I was alone with my anguish and memories. The knock at the door had startled me and I solemnly bade the caller to enter.

"Christina?" Madame Duchamp had called as she opened the door, "Did I wake you?"

"No, Madame, I was awakened by the rain," I replied, sitting up.

"Why don't you join us in the parlor," she requested, "you must be hungry."

"I don't feel very much like eating," I sighed.

"Well, at least join us for some tea?" she implored.

"Very well," I half-heartedly replied, "but first I would like a hot bath."

"I will have one of the servants prepare you a bath," she volunteered, "take your time."

She exited the room and I heard her summon one of Sir James' servants who entered a few moments later and proclaimed, "Your bath is ready, Mademoiselle Lafage."

I soaked in silence feeling a little more relaxed but even the comfort of the hot water could not dispel my grief.

I dressed and as I headed toward the parlor I could hear Madame Duchamp's voice, "I think it best if I take Christina back to France."

"You know that you and Christina are welcome to stay with us as long as you want," Sir James offered.

"Many thanks, old friend, but I think it would be better for Christina if we return to France," she affirmed.

"Understood," replied Sir James as I entered the parlor.

"Ah, Christina, we will be returning to France tomorrow morning," Madame Duchamp announced.

"As you wish," I replied sitting down next to her. It did not matter to me if we left or stayed. Nothing seemed to matter.

The conversation was interrupted by one of the servants who came to the parlor and apologetically said, "Beg your pardon, Sir, but there is a constable at the door who wishes to see you."

Sir James nervously looked at Madame Duchamp who calmly replied, "See how much he knows."

"Very well, Edward, show him in," Sir James instructed.

"It's probably just an inquiry," assured Madame Duchamp, "I hardly think they would send one constable for an arrest."

The constable entered the room and offered a polite greeting that seemed to put Sir James at ease.

"Good afternoon, would you like some tea?" Sir James offered.

"No, thank you," the constable replied.

"How can we be of service?" Sir James calmly asked.

"The town magistrate, William Moorsgate, has been reported missing and we found some . . . remains by an abandoned church not far from here. I was just wondering if any of you saw or heard anything strange last night," he asked.

"The remains you found were those of Moorsgate?" Sir James asked.

"Well, we aren't sure," the constable answered, "the remains were in such a state that they cannot be positively identified. I really don't want to go into too much detail in front of the ladies."

"Thank you, constable," Madame Duchamp smiled.

"I can assure you, we did not see or hear anything out of the ordinary last night," Sir James declared, shaking his head.

"Well then, I'll be on my way," he said, "sorry for the intrusion."

"Think nothing of it, let me show you out," Sir James volunteered.

"That was close," Rebecca said, relieved, "I was so nervous but you seemed so calm."

"It's all how you present yourself," Madame Duchamp answered.

Although I was present for the constable's visit and heard their conversation, I felt that I was outside looking in, just a disembodied spectator hovering just outside of what was going on.

"He was satisfied, I don't think he'll be back," Sir James announced as he entered the parlor.

"What a relief," Rebecca sighed.

Their conversation continued as I remained the quiet outsider, wrapped in my own veil of grief.

"Christina, are you with us?" Madame Duchamp gently asked, "you've been so quiet."

"I'm sorry, Madame, I am just . . . lost in thought," I sullenly replied.

"I know I don't have to ask you where your thoughts lie," she replied, gently stroking my hair, "but at least you can find some comfort knowing that the man responsible for Richard's death suffers the consequences of your own curse and will never find peace beyond the grave."

"It offers little consolation and will not bring Richard back to me," I tearfully replied.

"Christina," Sir James said, kneeling in front of me and taking my hand, "Just days ago, Richard told me that the time he had spent with you was the happiest he had ever known, and indeed I had never seen him happier. If you find comfort in nothing else, find it in what I have just related to you."

"Thank you, Sir James," I replied and tenderly kissed his cheek.

We had all retired soon after, but sleep did not come easy for me. I had never experienced the pain of loss before and I found it devastating. An uneasy sleep did come to me before dawn broke into another gray morning.

I dressed and walked outside, plucking a red rose from its thorny stem and headed for the cold place where my love slept. The rose that I had lain on the dirt seemed to be the only thing of beauty on the rough ground as my tears began to flow in the cloudy morning mist. About an hour had passed before I heard footsteps coming from behind me.

"It's never easy saying goodbye," said Madame Duchamp as I turned to face her, "I knew I would find you here."

"It's hard for me to believe he's really gone," I wept.

"I know, Christina," she whispered as I fell into her arms, "I know this weighs heavy on your heart, but be strong, my child."

"Your carriage is ready, Madame," I heard one of the servants announce.

"Come, Christina, we must go now," she said softly.

I turned for one last look at Richard's grave and tearfully whispered, "Farewell, my love."

Sir James and Rebecca were waiting beside the carriage as we approached. "Thank you for your hospitality, old friend, I wish our visit did not have to end on such a sad note," Madame Duchamp stated as she embraced Sir James, "My deepest sympathies are with you."

"Thank you, Madame," he replied and then turned to me, "I know that no words can ease your pain, but know that you and Madame Duchamp are always welcome here."

"You and Rebecca have been good to us," I replied, throwing my arms around him, "I will miss you."

We said our farewells and climbed into the carriage that whisked us off to the dock. As the boat sailed off across the channel, I longingly stared at the English shoreline. I was silent throughout the journey back to France and I was glad that Madame Duchamp did not press me for conversation.

Night had fallen as we found ourselves back on French soil and in a carriage bound for home. As the carriage came to a stop in front of the house and I climbed out, I caught sight of something out of the corner of my eye. I quickly turned to look, but whatever it had been was gone in an instant.

"What is it, Christina?" Madame Duchamp asked.

"Oh, I thought I saw something, but it was nothing," I sheepishly replied.

"You should get some rest," she suggested, "I know you haven't slept well."

Babette greeted us as we entered the house and I couldn't help looking over my shoulder just to prove to myself that I had not seen anything. Satisfied that nothing was out there, I closed the door behind me and concluded that grief and lack of proper sleep were causing me to see things.

"Welcome back, Mademoiselle Lafage," Babette smiled, "can I draw you a hot bath?"

"Yes, thank you, Babette," I wearily replied.

As I lay soaking, I tried to clear my mind and just relax when I heard a knock at the door.

"Enter," I bade as Madame Duchamp entered with a cup of tea.

"This will soothe you and help you sleep," she declared handing me the steaming cup.

"Thank you," I distantly replied.

"Christina," she began, "I know you are going through a lot right now and you need time to work through this, but don't let grief conquer you. I see so much potential in you, don't let that die."

"I am afraid the depths of sorrow have already conquered me and has laid waste to everything I had hoped for," I confessed.

"I know you are hurting right now . . . ," she said.

"It's tearing me apart!" I interjected, "Richard is gone and there was *nothing* I could do!"

"Christina that was not your fault," she consoled, "Richard is gone because William Moorsgate fatally shot him, there was nothing *anyone* could do."

"I miss him," I sobbed, "I've never missed anyone so much, not even my own parents."

"Don't let Moorsgate triumph by allowing sorrow to defeat you," she said as her eyes welled with tears, "I know you miss him and it grieves me to see you suffer so."

"I did not mean to upset you," I apologetically uttered.

"What hurts you, hurts me, Christina," she declared, "more than you know."

"But how . . . ," I started before she put her finger to my lips and said, "Drink your tea and get some rest. I know you haven't been sleeping well."

As she turned to go, I realized how close we had become since the day she found me in the wooded grove so many months ago.

I slowly sipped the tea she had given me and withdrew from the bath when I became sleepy. Whatever was in the tea had a powerful effect on me, for as soon as I crawled into bed I fell into the clutches of a deep, dreamless sleep.

I awoke to the late morning sun beaming through the slightly opened drapes, creating a warm glow. Sleep had left me feeling physically refreshed, but emotionally I was still drained. I crept out into the stillness of the hallway and headed for the kitchen as the smell of coffee wafted toward me. The kitchen was empty but the coffee was still hot enough to warm me as I contemplated what to do next. I was convinced that I could not continue on the path. The devastation that I felt was too much and I could no longer be a very eager student.

"Mademoiselle Lafage," Babette startled me, "Madame Duchamp has told me what happened in England. I am so sorry. Is there anything I can do for you?"

"No, Babette, thank you," I replied.

"You should at least eat something," Madame Duchamp suggested as she entered the kitchen.

"Well, maybe something light," I relented.

"Good," she sounded pleased, "you need to keep your strength up."

"Madame, I need to speak to you," I uneasily requested.

"I am here for you," she replied, placing her hands around mine.

"Madame Duchamp, I sincerely appreciate everything you have done for me, but I can no longer continue as your student. Richard's death has greatly distressed me to the point of being able to think of nothing else. I'm afraid I would make a poor student now and I do not wish to waste your time," I managed to finish before tears began streaming down my cheeks and I trembled in anguish.

"Christina, you are *not* a waste of time," she firmly stated, "and I have no intentions of dismissing you."

"But I would be of no use to you," I confessed.

"And what would you do, spend the rest of your life wallowing in sorrow?" she sadly asked, "Christina, when I first found you, an insatiable thirst for knowledge burned inside you, don't let that fire die. You have too much ahead of you to commit to a life of sorrow."

"But I loved him," I cried.

"Spending the rest of your life grieving is no way to honor someone's memory," she said, "and besides, I don't think Richard would have wanted that for you. I know you need time to get through this and I will support you and give you all the time you need, but remember, the journey does not end just because the road has darkened. Stay on the path, Christina, your Power is strong. Use it correctly and the world is yours."

I went for a walk in the garden and thought long and hard about everything Madame Duchamp had said to me. I missed Richard terribly, despite the short time we had been together. Did I really have the strength to get through this? Did I *want* to get through this? Madame Duchamp had taught me so much in the few months that I had been under her tutelage and even now in the depths of despair I could feel the Power within me, the same Power that had cursed my lover's killer and condemned his soul to eternal unrest.

I clutched Richard's onyx stone that hung around my neck and remembered one of the last things he had told me as he lay dying was to stay on the path, but could I overcome the pain and stay the course? I decided I would try, I knew it wouldn't be easy but Madame Duchamp was right, Richard would not want me to wallow in sorrow. I would keep his onyx stone around my neck and close to my heart always as a reminder and a source of inspiration. I would stay on the path – for Richard, for Madame Duchamp and for myself.

I did not realize how long I had been in the garden until I noticed the sunlight giving in to the dim of evening. My pace quickened as I neared the back door of the house and then a faint sound halted me. I quickly turned around and beheld the face of a watcher among the hedges. He quickly began to run but I would not let him get away as I started after him. When I could see him clearly, I stood still and commanded him to stop, concentrating my Power toward him. His running abruptly ceased, as he no longer had power over his own limbs.

"Turn around and come toward me!" I commanded. He slowly started toward me in disbelief and began uttering prayers. Still holding him in my Power, I led him back to the house and called for Madame Duchamp.

"Christina, I was beginning to worry," she said emerging from the house, "And who is this?"

"I found him in the garden, spying. And this is not the first time, is it monsieur?" I questioned.

"No, Mademoiselle Lafage, it is not," he nervously replied.

"Who are you and how do you know me?" I firmly asked.

"My name is Bouche, I was hired by your father to find you," he confessed as my father emerged from the shadows of the tall trees.

"Christina," he pleaded, "return home with me, your mother and I have been so worried and upset since you left."

"She is home!" Madame Duchamp broke in.

"I was not speaking to you, Madame, let Christina answer for herself," he sternly remarked.

"How dare you come to my home and address me in that manner!" she angrily shouted.

"Madame, please," I implored, "don't harm him." I could see the anger in her eyes and I knew she would have caused him great pain had I not intervened. "Father, please go," I told him, "I made my choice months ago and have no intention of returning with you."

"Christina, you are under that woman's influence, you don't know what you are saying," he insisted.

"I am well aware of what I say. I have learned many things and have had many experiences and I am no longer a child," I declared.

"Can't you see she wants nothing to do with you? Leave us!" Madame Duchamp exclaimed.

"I know you have cast some wicked spell over her where her will is not her own," he affirmed.

"Christina is here with me by her own choice. I cast no such spell. Leave now, for my patience with you grows thin!" she shot back at him.

"I will not leave without my child!" he shouted, "No matter what you . . . ,"

"She is not your child!" Madame Duchamp declared and I looked at my father in shock.

"What?" I gasped.

"Christina," Madame Duchamp nervously announced, "you are *my* child."

"Don't believe her, Christina, it's a devilish lie!" he tearfully shouted.

"Don't you think it's time she knew the truth?" she angrily insisted.

"Father," I confronted him, "if you have ever loved me, be truthful with me now."

"Christina," he softly uttered as he bowed his head, "my wife and I had no children of our own and we swore we would love you as our own and raise you in a Christian household . . . but you are not our flesh and blood."

The shock of what I had just learned had left me reeling, speechless and hurt. The parents that had raised me were not my own and the one person I had confided in and grown so close to had kept her real identity from me – her own child! At that point I did not want to be near either of them, so I ran into the growing darkness.

"Christina!" I heard Madame Duchamp shout as she started after me. I ran until I could run no more and collapsed into the damp grass, my chest heaving and my eyes blinded by tears. Moments later, Madame Duchamp tracked me down and sat down beside me.

"Why have you never told me?" I asked her through bitter tears.

"Christina, I am sorry," she began, "there were so many times I wanted to tell you, but the time just wasn't right and then Richard was killed, I did not want to strain your emotions any further. Believe me, this is not how I wanted you to find out."

"I still do not understand," I said wiping my tears.

"Come back to the house," she suggested, helping me to my feet, "I will explain everything to you."

As we drew nearer to the house, I could see that my father and his spy were still there and still trying to convince me to leave.

"Christina, I have raised you as my own and I implore you it is not too late to abandon this blasphemous path you have chosen and return with me," he asserted.

"I cannot," I forcefully replied, "I have made my choice, now please go and never return here."

"I will continue to pray for you," he said as he embraced me and then he and his spy reluctantly turned to go. Even though I had known him my entire life, he seemed like a stranger to me now and the feelings of alienation I had as a child all made sense to me now. I had never belonged with my adoptive parents in the village.

As I watched him go, I felt Madame Duchamp's hand on my shoulder as she whispered, "Come inside now, I have much to tell you." I followed her to the house and into the parlor where a warm fire was blazing in the hearth.

"I need answers," I requested, sitting down next to her.

"And you shall have them," she humbly replied. I took a deep breath, prepared for what answer I might receive and asked, "Who is my real father and why have you never told me?"

"I will tell you everything from the beginning," she proceeded, "I was very young when I was inducted into the Black Arts by my mother who had been inducted by her mother as it had been for generations. My father spent much of his time in Paris, so my mother basically raised me herself. There was a small band of villagers who held annual Black Masses outside of the village in secret, not far from the wooded grove where I found you. It was at one of these Black Masses where I met Jean Lafage, brother of the man who raised you and the village viceroy. The rest of the village, of course knew nothing of his sacrilegious exploits or his numerous affairs. He was much older than I when we began our affair and I knew I wasn't the only one he was with, but I was the only one to become pregnant. I met with him in secret in the grove the night I found out and when I told him I was carrying his child, he became furious. He ordered me to terminate the pregnancy, but I refused, which made him even angrier; Jean Lafage was accustomed to getting what he wanted. He stormed back to the village and would not see me again. I told no one who the father of my child was except for my parents who promised Lafage they would never divulge the identity of my child's father. The night you were born, Lafage came to our house with his henchmen and the clergy and arrested my parents and I for heresy. When my mother protested, he ran her through with his sword and ordered that she be burned. You were taken from me and brought to Lafage's brother to be raised as his own.

At the trial the next morning, my father was ordered to be tortured until he divulged the names of those in our circle. He never did and eventually died from the torture they inflicted upon him. I was livid that Lafage had betrayed me and killed my parents and it showed at my own trial when I divulged everything I knew about Monsieur Lafage to the magistrates, including the fact that he was the father of my child. He of course, denied everything and the magistrates believed him and sentenced me to burn at the stake for heresy at the setting of the sun. As they led me away, he said to me, 'You see, foolish girl, you can never get to me.'

His arrogance and betrayal made me so angry, I spat in his face and vowed revenge. He even went so far as to have all the members of our circle murdered so no one else could accuse him of any wrongdoing and saved his own cowardly hide. I sat in my cell as the day grew dim and simmered in anger waiting for the vengeance that would be mine. As the cell grew dark, I saw the outline of a tall figure in the corner. I squinted and tried to focus as Lucien emerged from the shadows.

He knelt down beside me and whispered, 'Lafage has killed my followers and betrayed me. He will feel my wrath through you, unleash the Power I have bestowed upon you.'

I looked into his dark eyes and replied, 'With pleasure.'

When I could no longer see the sun, I heard the sound of a key opening a lock as I stood to meet my escort. The acrid smell of burning flesh hung heavily over the village square as they had already burned members of our small circle that Lafage had murdered. I was led to the stake as Lafage preached his rhetoric about ridding the village of heretics and evil until I could stand no more.

I broke free of my escort and shouted, 'You filthy hypocrite! How can you condemn me for the very things that you have practiced?!'

'Be silent, wench!' he shot back, 'Pay no attention to the devil's lies.'

At that point I commanded the wind to rise and the thunder to roar, causing the spectators to run in fear.

Lafage remained, arrogant as ever, and replied, 'You cannot defeat me, Lucien would not leave me unprotected.'

'Lucien has already abandoned you,' I triumphantly stated. He looked at me in disbelief and raised his hand against the swelling storm to no avail. The rain now began to fall, light at first then as my anger swelled, so the rain fell heavier. He turned to run as I invoked the winds of the four directions to hold him fast and to wring and pull until he was in pieces and the rain fell red with blood. The cracking of bone was echoed in the thunder and the ripping of flesh was illuminated by the lightning.

That was the first time I had used the full extent of my Power and I was exhilarated as I let the bloody rain wash over me. At that point I resolved to learn as much of the Black Arts as I could and travel the world to gain knowledge."

I was enthralled by what she told me, but one question still burned inside of me and I put it to her, "Why did you not take me with you?"

"Christina, I had nowhere to go, no money and no means of support," she explained, "I did not wish to leave you behind, but I had no other choice. I gathered up what little I had and headed for Paris, but

I made a solemn promise to come back for you when I could give you everything you deserved. Fortunately, I was adept at making potions and able to earn barely enough to further my learning, but you were in my thoughts all the while. After years of traveling, I returned to Paris with the knowledge I had gained and discovered that the wealthy paid handsomely for the services I could provide. Not long after that, I gained the reputation and financial stability; it was then that I came for you."

"But how did you know where to find me or even what I looked like?" I curiously asked.

"From gazing into the crystal," she answered, "even though I couldn't be with you, I could still watch over you. All those nights you spent in the churchyard, you never really were alone."

My eyes grew wide and my jaw dropped, "You mean the watchful presence that I felt there was you?"

"Yes," she smiled, "I've watched you question authority, your parents' faith and I've watched you long for the things your family could not give you. It was very difficult for me, not being able to hold you or raise you as my own." She looked remorseful as she wiped away the tears that had welled in her eyes. "I hated keeping all of that from you. I feel better now that you know," she confessed.

"This is all so. . . . overwhelming," I excitedly replied, "I don't know what to say."

"I know it can't be easy for you, but you've always known you were different and destined for a greater purpose," she affirmed, "the blood of many generations of necromancers flows through your veins."

We talked well into the night as I tried to cope with who I really was. Even as a young child I always felt different, that I never really belonged, but all of those feelings had disappeared when Madame Duchamp had taken me under her wing. I came to realize that this was my rightful place and I would embrace my newly discovered heritage, but as exciting as discovering my identity had been, it made me miss Richard even more. Here it was, the most important secret that had ever been revealed to me and I could not share it with him. I fell silent and sullen as I thought of him and wiped the tears from my eyes.

The morning sun was on the horizon as I withdrew from the parlor and headed for my room. The events of the previous night had left me exhausted and in need of a long sleep.

5

It didn't take long for word to get around that Madame Duchamp and I had returned to France as clients were already at our doorstep. Most of them were simple potions and poisons, while others proved to be more interesting as in the case of Madame DuBoise, who came to us after she found out that her husband had been less than faithful.

"I want him deprived of sexual potency," she told Madame Duchamp and I.

"Won't you be depriving yourself?" I asked her.

"Christina, that's not your concern," Madame Duchamp gently scolded.

"That's quite all right," replied Madame DuBoise with a smile, "I have already taken a lover for myself."

"Very well," Madame Duchamp said, "bring me a lock of his hair and a strip of leather from something he has worn."

She returned about an hour later with the requested items and Madame Duchamp began to entwine the leather with the lock of hair.

"This is called the ladder," she explained to me, "it's a very effective impotency spell."

When the hair and the leather were one, she proceeded to tie nine knots in it and chant,

"A string of nine knots tied with care,

In a strip of leather entwined with hair,

And in nine knots it shall remain,

To cause strength and virility to wane."

She then handed it to Madame DuBoise and said, "The charm is set now; however, if the knots are untied, the spell will be broken."

"Thank you, Madame Duchamp," she replied as she handed her payment for the charm.

A steady stream of clients had kept us busy most of the day and I was relieved when the last of them had gone. Madame Duchamp had been instructing me and involving me more and more in the spell casting process from mixing the potions to chanting the spells. I sank into the sofa in the parlor and had just closed my eyes for a few seconds when Madame Duchamp entered and sat down next to me.

"It has been a long but profitable day and you have done very well," she complimented.

"Thank you . . . Mother," I affectionately replied.

"I've waited a long time to hear that from your lips," she said, embracing me. I felt that she needed to hear that from me as much as I needed to call her that. From the very first day I met her, I had sensed some sort of connection between us that surpassed teacher and apprentice.

"Pardon me, Madame," Babette interrupted, "but there is a man here to see you."

"One more, daughter?" Madame Duchamp asked me.

"One more," I agreed.

"Show him in, Babette," she instructed.

A tall, well-built man in his thirties and very well dressed entered the parlor and said, "Good evening, Madame Duchamp, Mademoiselle Lafage, my name is Devereux. I would like to employ your services."

"What can we do for you, Monsieur Devereux?" Madame Duchamp asked with a smile.

"I was slated to be appointed Captain of the Royal Guard by the king, but he has appointed another," he explained, "the man he appointed has whispered lies about me in the king's ear and cost me my rightful appointment. I want this man dead."

"You certainly get right to the point, Monsieur Devereux," Madame Duchamp replied.

"I don't believe in wasting time," he declared.

"Killing such a high-ranking official carries a very high price," she seriously stated.

"I don't care about the cost," he announced, "I want him to suffer and I will double your fee if you do this for me now."

"Well, Monsieur," she coolly stated, "if we were to do this for you we would require two things."

"Name them and you shall have them with all speed," he interrupted.

"We would need the cloak of your intended victim and a live black goat," she concluded.

"If you will give me one hour, they shall be yours," he decreed.

"Very well, one hour," she agreed.

"Thank you, ladies," he replied, "one hour, you have my word."

As he turned to go, Madame Duchamp whispered, "We need to prepare."

"Do you think it is wise to kill such a high-ranking official?" I asked, feeling uneasy.

"That just drives the price up," she smiled, "remember, don't let fear or doubt get the better of you. And besides, it will look like an accident."

Her reassurance and confidence put me at ease as I followed her down into the cellar where she lit some very strong incense.

"Christina, I want you to handle this," she confidently announced.

"Me?" I gasped.

"You have more than proved yourself over the past few months and I will be here to assist you," she assured.

"But . . ." I stuttered.

"This is not your first kill," she said, "I've seen what you can do."

"But that was done for vengeance, out of anger," I protested, "I have no animosity toward this man."

"That is why you must concentrate very hard and channel your energy into anger," she explained, "When you see your intended victim, visualize William Moorsgate or Leblanc and remember how it *felt*."

"I don't know if I can," I replied, "potions and poisons are quite easy, but this is another matter."

"For everything there is a first time and this will not be your first kill," she reminded me, "I *know* you can do this, have confidence in yourself."

As I sat down to meditate, I took a deep breath of incense-laden air and felt the Power stirring within me. If I were to be a master of the Black Arts, as I truly wanted to be, I would have to put fear and doubt aside and perform the task at hand. As I meditated and prepared myself for what I was about to do, I could feel the Power pulsating through my veins. I felt myself getting stronger and I distinctly heard Lucien's voice whisper to me, "Do it, Christina, it would serve me well."

My eyes abruptly shot open and brought me out of my meditative state.

"Are you ready, Christina?" Madame Duchamp quietly asked.

"I. . . heard Lucien's voice," I replied.

"You must obey the Master," she instructed.

"Then I am ready," I declared, rising to my feet. Lucien's words struck a chord deep within me and I would do my best to please him.

Monsieur Devereux was true to his word and returned in one hour with the requested items. The three of us then descended into the cellar to begin our dastardly mission.

"Use the bone-crusher spell, Christina," Madame Duchamp whispered, "and remember, the stronger your concentration and will, the stronger your Power will be."

She then took the crystal ball from the shelf and placed it at the edge of the long table and announced, "You may begin, Christina."

I nodded in agreement, spread the cloak of the Captain of the Royal Guard on the table, picked up the black goat and placed it in the middle of the cloak. The animal was very calm as it lay on top of the cloak and I stroked its soft, ebony coat.

"I thought you were to perform this spell, Madame Duchamp," Monsieur Devereux broke the silence.

"My daughter is quite capable, I assure you," she confidently replied as she handed me a sharp, red-handled dagger. The warm neck of the animal pulsated under the sharp blade that I placed against its throat as I prayed to Lucien for strength and made a clean cut. As the blood spurted from the animal's throat, I quickly grabbed a large silver bowl to catch it and held the open would over the bowl until it bled no more and the goat lay still. I then skinned and removed the bones, placing them in the center of the cloak and sprinkled them with the blood as I began the spell:

"Hear me, O Dark Lord,

Accept this sacrifice by my hand,

For you and your divine horde,

Who rule over this dark land."

"O'er this prey grant me power,

As blood anoints these bones,

Let the bell toll the final hour,

In low and mournful tones."

"Let he whose bones I smash,

Never again see the light of day,

And fires of Hell will burn to ash,

The life I now take away."

The crystal that Madame Duchamp had been gazing into had become cloudy and then revealed an image of a man riding on a horse – the Captain of the Royal Guard. She looked at me and nodded as I picked up a heavy wooden hammer, took a deep breath and brought it down with all my strength on the pile of bloody bones that lay on the cloak before me. The horse the man had been riding, apparently frightened by something unseen, suddenly threw his rider to the ground, shattering the rider's shoulder. I raised the hammer again, this time bringing it down on the leg bones as the man grasped his legs in pain. I followed suit on all of the bones until only the skull was left. A quick glance at the crystal showed that the Captain of the Royal Guard was on the ground writhing in pain from his shattered bones.

"Finish it, Christina," Madame Duchamp commanded. I thought about what she had said earlier about channeling my anger and thought of William Moorsgate as I brought the final crushing blow down on the skull. The familiar exhilarating rush of power ran through my body as I took the life of the Captain of the Royal Guard. It was as if his life force had become part of my own and made me stronger. I was not as bothered about taking a life as I thought I would be. I enjoyed the rush that enhanced my Power and I knew that I would kill again to sustain it. A surge of energy washed over me as I felt my temperature rise and I came to realize that I had become a cold-blooded killer . . . and I enjoyed it.

"Your spell has been cast, monsieur," I stated triumphantly, "The Captain of the Royal Guard is dead."

He had been looking into the crystal with Madame Duchamp and had witnessed the entire incident.

"You certainly do not disappoint, Mademoiselle Lafage," he smiled.

"I learned from the greatest authority," I replied as I looked over at Madame Duchamp.

"Well, I thank you for your services," he said, handing Madame Duchamp the fee he promised, "I trust you will tell no one what I have paid for."

"Of course not, Monsieur Devereux, we practice with the utmost discretion," she assured, "and may I be the first to congratulate you on your new position."

"Thank you, Madame Duchamp, and I owe it all to you and your lovely daughter," he replied as he kissed my hand.

"Your ambition has served you well, Captain," I stated.

"Indeed it has," he said, "but I think it would better serve me if I was at the king's side when he hears the news about the previous captain. Thank you again, ladies."

I could still feel the energy pulsating through me as I watched our guest leave and I wanted to go for a walk in the garden, but something was pulling me toward my room. I had no desire for sleep, yet I felt *something* waited for me beyond the door. I slowly turned the knob and entered as my eyes adjusted to the darkness. A flame suddenly flickered and began to dance on the candle that I kept beside my bed, illuminating Lucien's reclining figure. His dark hair spilled over his bare shoulders as he lay on my bed covered only by a thin sheet.

"Come to me," he seductively whispered. My energy instantly turned into a burning desire as I advanced toward the bed and sat down beside him.

"Have this evening's events pleased you?" I asked, caressing his lips.

"Immensely," he answered, stroking my cheek, "even now you must feel the Power coursing through your whole body."

"Absolutely, it's very stimulating," I replied as he leaned toward me for a sensual kiss. I ran my tongue over his lips and down his neck as his hands moved over my shoulders and began to undo and unfasten until I was out of my clothes. His sensual caresses sent me into ecstasy as I yearned to have him inside me. I lay back on the bed pulling him toward me, feeling his hot breath on my neck as he entered me. His slow penetrating motion prolonged my pleasure as I found his rhythm and moved with him as one.

"Lucien," I whispered as I felt the sensation mounting and becoming more intense with each movement until every part of me was seething in sensual climax. Even the rush of Lucien's icy seed did not seem to affect me as cries of pleasure erupted from deep within me.

"Your Power has become stronger," he declared as he withdrew, "I can feel it within you."

"When I performed the spell, I felt it wash over me like a wave of pure energy," I confessed.

"Every life you take will make your Power stronger and win my favor," he smiled, "but you still need to sleep. The sun will rise in a few hours and new opportunities will present themselves."

"Opportunities?" I asked.

"Sleep now," he said quietly as he closed my eyes and kissed my forehead.

I woke the next day, alone. Not that I expected to find Lucien lying next to me, his hypnotic presence was physically fulfilling, but I still felt emotionally empty.

I proceeded to the kitchen where Madame Duchamp was seated at the table gently tearing open an envelope.

"Good morning, mother," I yawned.

"Good afternoon," she smiled, "You had a guest last night?"

"Lucien," I answered, "he was waiting for me in my room."

"I see," she said, "I wondered why you went straight to bed. He must have been very pleased with your execution of the death spell."

"Yes, he was," I candidly replied.

"Having Lucien come to you after you've performed the death spell is a very high honor, Christina," she severely remarked.

"I meant no disrespect," I quickly apologized, "I am always honored by Lucien's presence and his compliments are *very* satisfying. It's just that . . ."

"What is it?" she asked, "you can tell me."

"My body and my soul belong to Lucien, but not my heart," I confessed.

"Richard," she softly said.

"Yes, I still miss him," I confided, wiping a tear from my eye, "The reason the death spell was so successful was because of him. I did as you suggested and channeled all of my anger and hurt and thought of William Moorsgate as I delivered the final blow."

"You harbor a lot of anger," she pointed out.

"Of course I have a lot of anger!" I cried, "Even though Moorsgate is dead by my hand it does not change the fact that he took Richard from me."

"Christina, your anger will serve you when you channel it in the right direction and it will strengthen your Power, but don't let it eat away at you," she advised. "Your anger is deadly, Christina; keep it in check or it will kill you."

"I am sorry, mother," I replied, "but I am still trying to work through this."

"It takes time," she said, grasping my hand, "be strong."

I noticed an envelope lying on the table and dimly inquired, "What have you there?"

"It arrived this morning," she replied with a hint of curiosity as she opened the envelope and pulled out what appeared to be an invitation. "It seems we are invited to a masquerade party this evening at the home of Michel LeDoux," she said cheerfully, "he's been a client for years."

"I would rather not attend," I sullenly replied.

"This would be good for you," she smiled, "you need a diversion."

"I. . . I don't know," I sighed.

"This is just what you need to lift your mood," she said persuasively, "come, you will see."

I reluctantly agreed and later found myself outside, mask in hand, with Madame Duchamp as a lavishly ornate carriage stopped in front of the house. As I climbed inside, I was hoping we would not stay long as I was not in a festive mood.

"Don't look so down," Madame Duchamp smiled, "you will have a good time."

"I will try," I half-heartedly replied.

The carriage pulled up in front of the LeDoux house and I could hear an orchestra playing in the distance. We entered the house and were led to the room where the orchestra was performing. The room itself was quite small compared to other ballrooms I had seen, but large enough to accommodate the orchestra and the guests. As I looked upon the masked guests and listened to the music, my sullen mood began to lift, so I donned my black velvet cat-eyes mask and joined the party. I had never been to a masquerade party and it did seem to be the diversion that I needed.

A man in an elaborate headdress with a snarling tiger's head and cape to match ambled toward us laughing, "I recognize you, Madame Duchamp, even through your feathered mask!"

"Monsieur LeDoux!" she exclaimed, "What a remarkable costume."

"And who is this lovely maiden at your side?" he asked.

"My daughter, Christina," she proudly answered.

"Mademoiselle," he smiled as he kissed my hand.

"It is a pleasure, Monsieur LeDoux," I politely responded.

"The pleasure is all mine," he announced as he linked arms with both of us and wandered about the room. Monsieur LeDoux shared the latest gossip with us about his guests, such as one of the queen's ladies-in-waiting, who wore butterfly wings on her back and an elaborate yellow wig, and was reputedly having an affair with one of the clerics.

"Do you see that man over there?" he asked, pointing to a man wearing a horse's head mask with a long flowing mane. "He has just been appointed Captain of the Royal Guard."

I recognized the man as Monsieur Devereaux and when our eyes met, he quickly looked away.

"The previous captain was killed in a tragic accident," he went on, "they say he was trampled by his own horse."

"Tragic," echoed Madame Duchamp as she shot a knowing glance in my direction.

As we strolled around the room listening to the swelling melodies of the orchestra, I looked around at the sea of masked faces. There were masks made from the finest silk and velvet fashioned into shapes such as suns, swans and crescent moons.

Men dressed as jokers in bright colors performed acrobatic feats while children dressed as cherubs laughed and tried to imitate them.

We talked and laughed with the rest of the guests until the stroke of midnight when cries of "Unmask! Unmask!" echoed through the room and all of the guests began to reveal themselves. Most of them I had recognized either as clients or from other parties we had attended.

A man whom I hadn't recognized timidly made his way over to Madame Duchamp and myself and very softly introduced himself, "Good evening, Madame Duchamp, Mademoiselle Lafage. My name is Stefan Janot, I am a friend of the Captain of the Royal Guard, and he suggested I speak to you."

"What can we do for you, Monsieur Janot?" asked Madame Duchamp in her usual professional manner.

"Can we go outside to talk?" he shyly asked, "It's a bit noisy here."

"As you wish," she smiled as we withdrew from the warmth of the party and into the chilly night air. I desperately wanted to go back inside as the cold wind made me shiver, but there was business to be discussed and my comfort would have to wait.

"I believe I have need of your services," he announced.

"Go on," she encouraged.

"My late wife, Gabrielle, has been visiting me in dreams," he explained, "it seems she is trying to tell me something, but I always awaken before the message comes through. Is there a way you can contact her?"

"How long has she been dead?" Madame Duchamp inquired.

"About one month," he answered.

"One month," she said pensively, "it will be difficult, but it can be done . . . for the right price."

"You shall have it," he replied satisfied, "When can you do this for me?"

"Come to us nine days from now in the thirteenth hour," she instructed.

"Thank you for your time, ladies," he politely stated as we made our way back inside.

"Let us enjoy the rest of the party, Christina," Madame Duchamp advised, "for tomorrow and the eight days that follow we become one with the grave."

The party lasted for hours after our meeting with Monsieur Janot and as we made our way home later, I could just see the first light of dawn. I watched the sunrise from my window before crawling into bed, since it would be the last I would see for the next nine days. As the sun spread its rays over the garden, I thought of Richard and how we had watched many sunrises before drifting into slumber in each other's arms.

"I miss you, my love," I whispered as I closed the drapes, climbed into bed and let sleep overtake me.

I awoke to a darkened house and burning incense – the preparation had begun; nine days of bland food, darkness and meditation. The days seemed to drag as we took on the dismal mood of the grave.

Finally, the ninth day came upon us and Madame Duchamp came to get me to get everything ready before the arrival of Monsieur Janot. I descended the stone steps into the cellar and gathered everything we would need for the night's work.

"Do you have everything we need?" Madame Duchamp asked as I ascended the stone staircase.

"Yes," I confidently answered, "incense, herbs, candles, skull and of course the Grand Grimoire."

"And you remember how to use them and everything I have taught you?" she tested.

"Yes," I answered, preparing myself for what I thought was going to be a last-minute examination of my knowledge of necromancy.

"Excellent," she smiled, "but this time you will not be assisting me."

I was stunned as feelings of disappointment welled up inside me. Why would she have me go through all the preparation only to tell me I would not be needed? "As you wish," I replied, my voice echoing my disappointment, "If you would rather do this alone . . ."

"Oh, I will not be alone, I will be with you," she assured.

My disappointment had now turned to confusion. "But you just said you do not need me to assist you with raising the dead."

"I will not be raising the dead, Christina," she declared, "you will."

"*I* will?" I asked, stupefied.

"Yes," she replied confidently, "you've done potions, poisons, and even the death spell. This is the next logical step for you. Just remember everything I have taught you and show no fear."

I felt honored that she had so much confidence in my Power, but at the same time I was frozen with fear -- not fear of the dead, but the fear of *failure*. I did not want to let Madame Duchamp down, especially not in front of a client.

"But what if I can't?" I nervously asked.

"If you believe you can't, then you will fail," she bluntly stated, "You must have confidence."

"I don't think I am ready," I confessed.

"You *are* ready," she knowingly replied, "trust my judgment and have faith in your Power."

I heard a knock at the front door and a moment later Babette came into the kitchen and announced that Monsieur Janot had arrived. Madame Duchamp placed her hand on my cheek and said, "You will be so busy performing the ceremony that you will not have the time to doubt yourself. Now cast your fear and doubt aside. I will be right there beside you."

The three of us walked to the cemetery in the crisp night air as I tried to quell my fear of failure by mentally going over every part of conjuring the dead. We approached a large stone crypt fastened with a slightly rusted metal lock. As Monsieur Janot removed a key from his pocket, I remembered the strong odor of decay that erupted from crypts and prepared for the worst. The lock clicked as the key turned and the heavy door swung open, releasing the pungent stench of death. Monsieur Janot reeled and began to wretch as the fetid air entered his lungs.

"I am sorry," he apologized, "I should have expected this."

He regained his composure and we entered the crypt where the first thing I did was light the incense and inhale deeply. Madame Duchamp helped set everything up as she instructed Monsieur Janot to open his wife's coffin. He seemed hesitant at first and then took a deep breath and slowly raised the lid.

"Oh, Gabrielle!" he cried, turning away in horror.

Madame Duchamp went over to him, put her arm around his shoulders and sympathetically whispered, "It is never pleasant to look upon the face of the dead, but it must be done."

"I cannot bear to look at her," he muttered.

"We will work as quickly as we can, but you have to be the one to ask why she haunts your dreams," Madame Duchamp explained.

"If it must be done," he sighed, lowering his head. He maneuvered the coffin so the corpse's head pointed toward the east as I drew a circle in the damp earth of the crypt and inscribed it with the names of the demons from the <u>Grand Grimoire</u>. With dagger in hand, I walked over to where the corpse lay in its wooden box and was horrified by its appearance. I had seen but a few corpses, but never in the state of decay that Gabrielle Janot was in. I could see why her husband was so upset; the face, or what was left of it, had been gnawed by rats and insects, making it almost impossible to behold. The stomach had exploded, leaving a gaping hole writhing with maggots clinging to bits of bone and tissue, but as horrifying as it was, I also felt a sort of fascination at peering inside a human body.

I stared at it for several minutes before Madame Duchamp came over to me and whispered, "Christina, we are waiting."

"Do you think it will rise?" I asked, directing her gaze to the decayed corpse.

"The body is quite decayed, but it can be done," she confidently answered.

"Then let us begin," I said as she and Monsieur Janot entered the circle I had drawn in the dirt. I took the dagger and dragged the cold blade across my left hand, leaving a clean cut letting the blood drip into what was left of the corpse's mouth and then joined Madame Duchamp and Monsieur Janot in the circle.

Madame Duchamp handed me the <u>Grand Grimoire</u> and I began to read, "Lord of the darkness, let the body of Gabrielle Janot accept the

sacrifice of my blood, that her spirit return to this flesh and speak to us."
I waited, but the corpse did not stir. I felt my temperature rise with em-
barrassment as I quickly tried to figure out what went wrong.

"A true master would not let a mere corpse make a mockery of her
Power," Madame Duchamp whispered in my ear. But what was I to do?
I had followed the procedure to the letter, yet the corpse remained mo-
tionless. "We are waiting, Christina," Madame Duchamp impatiently
reminded.

Why did she not help me? She said she had complete faith in me
and now it seemed she had none. Had she done this on purpose? Did
she *want* me to fail? I felt so betrayed that I wanted to cry, but I would *not*
give her the satisfaction of showing any weakness as my anger began to
surface. I stared hatefully at the lifeless corpse and forcefully shouted,
"Hear me, all you spirits who ride the night wind, I command you to
bring forth the spirit of Gabrielle Janot to this lifeless corpse so that it
may rise and serve me!"

At that moment I felt the Power stirring within me as a cold wind
swept through the crypt and the rotting corpse began to rise. It slowly
stood up, turned toward me with maggots spilling from its exploded entrails and angrily asked, "Who are you, arrogant brat, to summon my
spirit into this rotten mass?!"

"My name is Christina Lafage," I fearlessly answered, not letting myself be intimidated, "I summoned you at the request of your husband!"

"Stefan?" her tone softened as she directed her gaze to the man
standing behind me.

"Gabrielle," he said with a quivering voice, "is it really you?"

"Stefan, I don't want you to see me this way," she stated sadly.

"Believe me, I did not wish to disturb your rest, but there is something
you have been trying to tell me, isn't there?" he asked, wiping away tears.

"Yes," she replied, her tone became serious, "the woman who offers
you comfort since my death is not the friend she pretends to be."

"But Marie's friendship has helped to ease the pain of your untimely
passing," he protested.

"Does it also help to ease her conscience?" she asked.

"I do not understand," Monsieur Janot replied, puzzled.

"She is the reason my body lies rotting in this crypt. Her desire for you has turned her into a murderer."

"We are just friends, as we all were, Gabrielle," he explained, "nothing more, and was it not she who cared for you when you fell ill?"

"Yes," she replied, "and it was also she who made me ill by slowly poisoning me and laughing as I lay dying."

"Poison!" he gasped.

"Yes, poison," she echoed, "so she could have you."

Monsieur Janot became furious. "Could this be true?" he asked Madame Duchamp.

"The dead have no reason to lie," she replied.

"Believe me, my husband," Gabrielle affirmed, "I've seen what is in her heart, and she is a cold-blooded murderer."

"Thank you, my love. Marie will pay dearly for this," he sternly replied.

"I would like very much to return to my rest, Mademoiselle Lafage," Gabrielle requested, "but first, I would like to reward you for helping my husband contact me."

"You are very kind, Madame Janot," I politely replied, "but what I want you cannot give me."

"Oh, but I can," she insisted, "I know that your lover dwells in the land of the dead now, but there is a way to cross the barrier and bring him back."

"Go on," I was astounded.

"There are certain incantations to conjure a spirit guide that can take you to the land of the dead and release your lover from death's icy grip."

"What incantations must be spoken?" I excitedly asked.

"Your mother knows well the incantations that I speak of, but they must not be spoken here, only far to the east in the land of the pharaohs," she answered.

"But where in Egypt?" I implored.

"I can tell you no more, the rest of the journey is for you," she affirmed, "now release my spirit from these decayed remains."

"Thank you, Madame Janot, I am grateful for the information you have given me. Go now and return to your rest; I'll not disturb you again," I assured.

"Farewell, Stefan," she sadly uttered, "heed my warning."

"I will, my beloved wife," he tearfully replied.

The corpse of Gabrielle Janot took one last breath and collapsed into the wooden coffin from which it rose.

I stood in the circle for several minutes absorbing what the spirit had revealed to me until Monsieur Janot broke the silence.

"Mademoiselle Lafage, I want Marie Marceau dead, but I want her to suffer for all the pain she has inflicted upon my wife!"

"Christina," Madame Duchamp called, but I did not answer.

"My apologies, Monsieur Janot," she said, "Come to us tomorrow evening with something personal from the one you wish dead and we will be able to help you."

"Thank you for a most informative evening," he replied handing her a large bag of coins. He placed Gabrielle back into her coffin as I silently helped Madame Duchamp pack up our equipment. The three of us exited the crypt and Monsieur Janot replaced the padlock on the heavy iron door. The outside air felt refreshing despite the cold and I drew in a long breath to clear my lungs.

"Tomorrow evening, then," Madame Duchamp reaffirmed.

"I will be there," Monsieur Janot sternly replied.

I kept silent as we walked home in the cold night air. I was still annoyed that Madame Duchamp did not help me earlier or tell me about the spell to free Richard. I purposely kept two paces ahead of her as I marched toward the house. I knew eventually I would have to speak to her, but at that moment I couldn't, as I was still seething with anger as I flung the door open and entered the house.

"Christina, stop!" I heard her shout from behind. Her irate tone had stopped me in my tracks and sent a bolt of fear through me, but I would not show my fear as I turned to face her.

"You will tell me what the problem is, now!" she severely stated folding her arms across her chest.

As much as I tried not to cry, I could not hold back my anger and my hurt. "Why did you not help me when I needed it?" I shouted through burning tears.

"I did help you," she answered, "you were not being forceful enough and I knew if I raised your ire a bit you would be more assertive, and you were! Necromancy is not a simple spell; if you are not forceful, it will not be effective."

So she did help me after all, but there was still the spell she never told me about.

"And what of these incantations that Madame Janot spoke of? Why have you never told me?" I furiously asked.

"Christina," she started as she approached me, "I would never put you in any situation where my confidence in you was not strong . . . or in any situation where I could lose you."

"Lose me?" I curiously asked.

"What Madame Janot spoke of is very dangerous and requires strict control. I cannot allow you to attempt it," she firmly stated.

"But I have control," I protested, "Did I not prove that tonight?"

"You still required my help to gain that control and if you cross into the land of the dead, you would be on your own. I could not go with you," she explained, "As advanced as you are, there are some things you are still not ready for."

But all of her warnings and explanations could not dissuade me; I would find out everything I needed to know and journey to Egypt myself if need be. "Teach me, then," I begged.

"No, it is much too dangerous," she flatly replied.

"Why would you deny me?" I cried.

She took me into her arms and held me as she whispered, "You are my daughter. I love you and I will not lose you again."

"Mother," I began, "I love you and understand you want to safeguard me from danger, but please, I *need* to do this."

"Christina, you know I would never deny you anything, but I cannot let you do this," she tearfully replied.

I took a deep breath and roused enough courage to firmly state, "I would prefer to do this with your help, but if I must, I will go alone."

"You have your father's stubbornness," she pointed out, "and you have no idea what you are getting yourself into."

"I am ready to take the risk and face whatever danger lies ahead," I declared.

"Christina, you could lose your Power or even your life," she cried, "You would take that risk for Richard?"

"Yes," I emphatically replied.

After a long pause, she reluctantly stated, "Very well, then, I will help you but I am still strongly opposed to this. If your mind is set on doing this, I would rather help you than have you attempt it on your own. But once you cross the barrier you will be on your own."

"Why can you not go with me?" I asked.

She lowered her head and responded, "Because I have already been there and I cannot go back."

"What do you mean? Tell me," I pleaded. I wanted to know what to expect.

"Quite a few years ago, a man came to me and asked if there was a way of bringing the dead back to life," she began, "I had known of the spell and how dangerous it was, so I told him I knew of no such thing, but he was persistent and offered me an immense fortune, so I agreed."

"Who did he want to return?" I asked.

"His six-year-old son who was taken prematurely by a fever," she continued, "We sailed to Egypt where I performed the spell and entered the land of the dead. There is a demon who rules over the dead, Abaddon, and it is him you must beware of. In order for you to free someone you must make a deal with him, but he will try to trick you and this is where you must be on your guard. I was not fortunate enough to have the guidance of someone with experience so I didn't expect to be deceived. He said he needed a sacrifice and my blood would do. I remember it clearly, 'Just a little,' he said, 'Just enough for a taste and I will let the boy go.' I relented as he wrapped his scaly arms around me and imbedded his sharp teeth into my neck. At first there was something erotic about it and I even enjoyed the first few moments, but I soon began to feel weak and realized that as my blood drained, my Power was draining with it. I struggled and tried to free myself, but he held tight and would not let go. I had never before been afraid of any situation I faced, but at that moment I knew what sheer terror felt like."

"How did you escape?" I gasped.

"I almost did not escape and thought I would spend eternity in the arms of the guardian of the dead, but as I became weaker I noticed a singular pulsating vein in his neck. The deeper he drank, the quicker it pulsated, and I realized it must be my Power flowing through it. I roused what strength I had left and lunged forward, driving my teeth into the throbbing vein. A warm rush of my own blood and the electrifying surge of Power filled my mouth and I began to regain my strength as Abaddon wailed in pain. My blood, mingled with demon's blood, gave me an incredible feeling of strength as I continued to drink making him weaker until I was completely revitalized. Abaddon's weakened corpse crumbled to the ground as I grabbed the child and ran while his vow of revenge echoed in my ears. We made it back safely and my Power was still intact but the whole experience damn near killed me. Now, knowing what you will face, I beg you to reconsider."

Her experience was truly terrifying and I would be lying if I said that I had no fear, but even after hearing of her almost deadly encounter, I felt that I still had to go through with it. "I hate to go against your wishes, Mother, but I cannot reconsider," I declared, "I must do this."

She put her arms around me and hugged me tightly, "You will have only one chance to free Richard; use all of your resources wisely. There will be no elixirs or potions I can administer to safeguard you. Everything will be up to you alone."

"I understand," I replied. "Will Abaddon ask for blood?"

"I don't know," she answered, "but he will ask for something and then try to trick you."

I looked into her eyes and confidently said, "I have received my Power directly from the master and have learned to use it from the greatest teacher . . . and I have a few tricks of my own." I knew this was difficult for her and my words did little to put her at ease, but I was also trying to convince myself that I could go through with it. My will was certainly strong enough, but did I have the courage? I would have to be strong; if I failed, I would also fail Richard and Madame Duchamp as well as myself and I was prepared to do anything to prevent that from happening.

"We will leave for Egypt as soon as our business with Monsieur Janot is finished," Madame Duchamp announced, "we still have to perform the death spell for him."

"I want to do it," I firmly stated.

"Then you shall," she smiled.

I wanted the familiar rush of power that came with executing the death spell as well as the experience. With every spell I performed, I felt my Power getting stronger and I needed all the strength I could muster to cross the barrier and free Richard.

It was another late night for us as I witnessed another sunrise before retiring. Once again my thoughts turned to Richard but it wasn't a tear of sadness that I shed, but one of joy as I silently whispered, "Soon, my love," and drifted into slumber.

6

I awoke the next day, refreshed yet anxious to work the evil magic that would give me the surge of Power I craved and build up my strength. I joined Madame Duchamp in the kitchen where the afternoon sun was casting long shadows through the open curtain.

"I have sent Babette to gather information on ships leaving for the Mediterranean," she solemnly said, "You should start packing."

"Mother, I am sorry about last night. I should not have gotten angry with you. I know you were trying to protect me," I said apologetically.

"You were justified, Christina," she confessed, squeezing my hand, "I did promise to teach you everything, but I still keep hoping you will reconsider."

"I cannot," I sorrowfully replied, "but I swear I will return with my life and my Power intact."

Monsieur Janot appeared at our door that evening eager to begin, so we adjourned to the cellar where the spell was to be performed. "I don't want her dead right away," he announced, "I want her to suffer."

I was a bit disappointed, as I really wanted to perform the death spell, I wanted to take her life and feel her life force within me.

"Have you something personal from your victim?" I asked.

"I have an undergarment smeared with her blood," he triumphantly replied as he threw it onto the table. Menstrual blood - very powerful indeed.

Madame Duchamp placed the crystal ball on the table as I grabbed a waxen image and wrapped it in the bloodstained cloth.

"How will I know when this will take effect?" he asked.

"Gaze into this crystal and you will see the spell at work," Madame Duchamp confidently replied.

When all was quiet, I began,

"Let this image of wax become Marie Marceau,

Let it be she to suffer and die slow,

No relief will she have from the pain,

That is certain to drive her insane."

The clouds in the crystal ball began to clear and reveal the image of Marie Marceau as I held a long needle over the candle flame until it glowed red-hot and slowly placed it on the shoulder of the waxen image. As the wax melted under the burning needle, Marie screamed and grabbed at her shoulder, tearing her clothes to reveal an open sore. I pierced every part of the waxen image with the needle until Marie was covered in burning sores and screaming from the pain.

Monsieur Janot watched his former friend and confidant with horror as he gazed into the crystal.

"How long do you want her to suffer?" I asked in a devious tone.

"My wife lingered for six days before she died. Six agonizing days; I want her to suffer the same," he insisted.

I took a deep breath of the incense-filled air and continued,

"The agony of these burning sores,

For six days shall be yours,

Neither day nor night will bring respite,

Until death comes to end your plight."

I looked up at Monsieur Janot whose eyes were still fixed on the suffering image in the crystal. "The spell is cast," I announced, "She will suffer for six days before death comes for her."

"Thank you, ladies," he uneasily replied as he left a sack of coins on the table.

We climbed the stone steps to the kitchen where Monsieur Janot nervously said he had to leave and exited through the back door. He looked pale and full of fear as he left and I asked Madame Duchamp, "Whatever came over him?"

"Monsieur Janot has led a life of privilege and I doubt he has ever seen true suffering," she answered, "I would not be at all surprised if he returned and wanted the spell reversed."

Madame Duchamp's assessment of Monsieur Janot's character was correct, for three days later he was at our door with tears in his eyes.

"Mademoiselle Lafage, you must remove the curse I asked you to put on Marie Marceau. It weighs heavy on my soul and I cannot bear to see her suffer any longer."

"Did you forget what she did to your wife? How she made her suffer?" I reminded him.

"No, I have not forgotten, but vengeance does not belong to me. I have no right to play God, only He can punish Marie. What I asked you to do was out of anger, I do not want this on my conscience."

"But Monsieur," I said to the weak-willed man before me, "what I have done I cannot undo. The curse must run its course."

"There must be some way," he pleaded.

"Perhaps," I replied pensively, "but it will be costly."

"Please," he begged, "I will pay whatever you ask."

I felt a sense of pride as I negotiated my first deal, after all, passage to Egypt was expensive, why not let it be funded by this man's desperation and guilt? "There is only one way," I declared, "I would have to kill her."

He lowered his head and sighed, "Very well, if it will end her suffering."

It would end her suffering . . . and strengthen my Power. Madame Duchamp had kept silent, but I knew she would have intervened had I needed her to.

Once again we descended the stone steps into the cellar where the waxen image still lay on the table wrapped in its bloody cloth.

"Marie has suffered so much because of my rage," Monsieur Janot tearfully confessed, "can you at least make her death swift?"

"As you wish," I replied opening the Grand Grimoire. I found the spell I was looking for and lit a long black candle with a slight gesture of my index finger as Madame Duchamp placed a large bell and the crystal ball on the table. I closed my eyes and took several deep breaths to focus my concentration and then began to read from the Grand Grimoire,

"Marie Marceau, I hereby sentence you to death,

That you draw your last breath,

At the sound of the tolling bell,

And the sight of this flame I will expel."

"I free your soul to go where it will,

And leave your body cold and still,

To strengthen my Power, I take your life,

And put an end to your suffering and strife."

I then closed the book and struck the bell as if tolling a knell for the dead and extinguished the candle flame between my fingers as I quickly glanced over at the crystal and saw Marie Marceau collapse as soon as the light disappeared from the candle. The rush of Power came as her life force became part of my Power, but it did not feel as strong as the other lives I had taken. Surely she was dead as I could plainly see in the crystal, but it was not the overwhelming rush I had expected.

"It is done," Madame Duchamp said to Monsieur Janot, who had kept his eyes closed through the whole ceremony.

"Is she . . . ?" he quietly asked.

"She has been released," Madame Duchamp answered.

"Praise God," he replied as he drew a dagger from underneath his cloak.

"What is the meaning of this?" Madame Duchamp demanded.

"My soul will surely burn in torment for what I have done, but I pray I can redeem myself in the eyes of God by destroying the devil's minions!" he shouted as he raised the dagger and lunged toward Madame Duchamp who quickly grabbed his wrist and squeezed until the dagger fell from his hand.

"You have no idea who you are dealing with," she laughed.

"I will kill you both!" he angrily shot back at her as they struggled, but the vice-like grip she still had on his wrist forced him to his knees.

"You should not make threats you cannot carry out," she teased.

"I will see you in hell!" he angrily snorted.

"You will be as weak in hell as you are on earth," she taunted, "some man you are." She looked over at me with a sardonic smile, "Take him, Christina."

I picked up the dagger and held it to his throat. "And just who were you going to kill?" I taunted, "I could slit your throat in an instant."

"Then do it and be done with me," he quivered.

"Oh, that's much too easy," I replied, "Tell me, are you feeling the same rage now that you felt when you asked me to make Marie Marceau suffer?"

"The only rage I feel is toward myself for asking for such a sin," he confessed.

I took the blade away from his throat, bent down and whispered in his face, "Does it make your blood boil?"

Tiny beads of sweat began to appear on his forehead and his face was flushed. "What are you doing to me?" he nervously asked.

"Is the rage burning inside you?" I continued as he began sweating profusely, "Do you feel your temperature rising to a fever pitch?"

"Stop!" he screamed as his skin began to turn a deep shade of red and I could feel the heat emanating from his body. Madame Duchamp quickly let go of his wrist as his skin became too hot to touch and began to blister and blacken from the heat. He screamed and writhed on the floor as the heat burned through his body until he was a smoldering lump of blackened flesh and when the life left his body, I felt it hit me like a bolt of lightning and strengthen my Power.

When the rush ended, I felt invincible and I wished I could go to the land of the dead at that moment. I certainly felt ready to face any demon I had to bargain with to free Richard, but Madame Duchamp soon brought me back to reality, "Christina, we must dispose of the body."

I helped her dump the blackened remains of Stefan Janot into the acid pit and watched as it bubbled and consumed the charred carcass.

"You did very well this evening," Madame Duchamp complimented, "You are refining your skills and harnessing the Power beautifully."

"Thank you, Mother," I humbly replied, "but there is one thing I do not understand."

"What is it, child?" she asked.

"When I performed the death spell and took Madame Marceau's life, the rush of power was weak, I barely felt it; with Monsieur Janot's death, it was much stronger," I replied.

"That is because Marie Marceau was weak with suffering, her life-force was waning. Monsieur Janot was healthy with a strong life force," she explained, "the rush is more powerful when a strong life-force is violently taken."

"His life was worth taking since I did not get paid for my work," I grumbled.

"But you negotiated the deal competently. Either you take their money or you take their life," she smiled.

The next few weeks we busied ourselves with preparing for the journey that would reunite me with Richard. Madame Duchamp was teaching me all she could remember about the land of the dead and what to expect, but despite her brave façade, I knew she was fearful of what lay ahead for me and I must confess, so was I. The thought of being with Richard kept my determination strong as I studied and memorized incantations on everything from the <u>Grand Grimoire</u> to the <u>Egyptian Book of the Dead</u>, which Madame Duchamp constantly tested my knowledge of until they became second nature to me.

"There is one more book I want you to read," she said as she led me upstairs to the attic and over to a forgotten trunk covered with dust and cobwebs. She produced a key from her pocket and with great difficulty opened the rusted lock. "This book has lain in this trunk for many years," she confessed, "I never thought I would have need of it again."

"What is it?" I curiously asked. "It is called <u>Descent Into Nekyia</u>," she replied, removing the dust-covered book from the trunk. "It was written centuries ago by a man named Salaam Ra-Khamin," she explained, "an Egyptian master obsessed with the land of the dead. He journeyed there and wrote of his experience on a papyrus scroll, explaining how the journey should be undertaken. He is also said to have written the <u>Egyptian Book of the Dead</u>."

"How did you come to have this book?" I inquired.

"It has been passed down through the ages, no one knows who translated it into French," she replied.

"And what of the original scroll?" I asked, fascinated.

"The priests of Egypt held it in such high regard it was the first scroll rescued from the Alexandrian library when the Romans burned it. Some say to destroy this scroll was the real reason the Romans started the fire, but it was kept in a secret location in the library and quickly relocated. It remains in Egypt, well hidden and very few have laid eyes on it," she concluded.

"But why would the Romans want to destroy such a valuable document?" I asked.

"They thought it a blasphemous document. They believed that mortals had no place in the land of the dead," she answered.

I studied the book intensely, memorizing incantations and gaining knowledge through the author's experience. I knew despite everything I had read and what I had learned from Madame Duchamp that knowledge is no substitute for experience. I was sure my experience in the land of the dead would be mine alone and I would have to face the demon Abaddon not knowing what he would ask of me. No matter what incantations I uttered, I would still have to bargain with him and the bargain changes for each traveler, and as I learned from Salaam Ra-Khamin's book, some never return to tell what they were asked.

7

The morning of our departure had finally arrived and I woke at dawn, anxious and well prepared. We would journey eight days by private carriage south to Toulon where we would board a ship bound for the warm waters of the Mediterranean. It would be a long journey and I was excited about seeing something of the world.

The trip through the French countryside was beautiful despite the bumpy ride on the rough roads and changing horses every twelve miles. The inns took some getting used to, as I had grown accustomed to the finest lodgings, which the average country inn did not provide.

We reached Lyons on the sixth day, just as the sun was beginning to set. Fortunately, the inn where we stopped wasn't crowded, save for a band of rowdy Englishmen on the "Grand Tour." As we entered the tavern, I could feel their eyes on us and hear their faint whispers as we walked past them to a table in the corner. I was neither fearful nor intimidated by their presence, as I knew Madame Duchamp carried a small pistol and I a dagger and we both had the advantage of using the Power.

One particularly drunken Englishman, very well dressed and obviously pampered his entire life, stumbled over to our table and began to flirt in his awkward French, "May I join you lovely ladies this evening? You look as though you have need of some company."

"No thank you, monsieur," Madame Duchamp politely replied, "we are fine on our own."

"Oh, but it is much too dangerous for two women to travel alone, you should travel with us," he said motioning to his friends who were watching with amusement and spurring him on.

"We have our own driver and are quite capable of taking care of ourselves," I smiled.

"So you appear to be," he said as he sat down next to me with his tankard of ale and then leaned toward me and whispered, "I have a private room where I could take good care of you, mademoiselle . . . all night long."

Before I could react, he slipped his hand between my thighs and ran his tongue down my neck as his drunken friends clapped and cheered. He was very drunk indeed as even the sting of my open palm across his face did not seem to sober him.

"That's what I love about French women, so fiery!" he exclaimed as he quickly picked me up and slammed me on the table just as I heard the click of a pistol's trigger being cocked.

I looked up and saw the barrel of Madame Duchamp's pistol pressed against my assailant's left temple as she scoffed, "Let my daughter go or this fiery French woman will splatter your brains all over this tavern." He began to shake as he nervously backed away from the table with the pistol still aimed at his head. "Are you all right, Christina?" she asked, never taking her eyes from the culprit.

"I am fine, Mother," I replied complacently, getting up from the table.

"M-my deepest apologies, ladies," he stammered, suddenly finding the sobriety that had eluded him earlier, "I have had too much to drink this evening."

"Is that the only reason that I should not pull this trigger?" she taunted.

"Please, Madame, I beg you," he implored with quivering voice.

"On your knees," she commanded in a serious tone, but despite her manner I knew she was toying with him, so I went along with the charade trying my hardest not to laugh out loud.

As he slowly fell to his knees, the once rowdy Englishmen now begged for their friend's life, one in particular who looked to be a bit older than the rest pleaded, "Madame, please, we are very sorry. If you spare our friend's life, we will leave."

She looked down at the nervous Englishman on his knees who had since wet himself, lowered the pistol and smirked, "Go on home to your mother, boy."

"Th -thank you, Madame, and once again, my apologies," he said as he rejoined his friends and they made a hasty retreat for the door of the tavern.

"Thank you, Mother," I calmly said, "but I was perfectly capable of handling a drunken Englishman."

"I know you were," she smiled, "but why should you have all the fun?"

Our driver, Gerard, who had been outside through the whole affair entered the tavern with a bemused look on his face and asked, "Is everything all right, Madame Duchamp?"

"Everything is fine, Gerard," she answered with a smile, "but we will not be spending the night here."

"As you wish, Madame," he replied, "There are a few more inns outside of town."

"Why can we not stay?" I asked, "The Englishmen have gone."

"They may return and I don't feel like sleeping with one eye open tonight," she replied.

We finished our meal in the tavern without incident and made our way to another inn for the night.

"Do you think the rest of our journey will be as eventful as tonight has been?" I jokingly asked.

"Who can say?" she laughed, "The world is full of obnoxious tourists." The trip had become a bit dull and the incident in the tavern had been an amusing diversion.

"We will reach Toulon the day after tomorrow," she said in a more serious tone, "from there we depart for Naples." She sat down on the rough straw mattress on the bed, looking down at the floor as she whispered, "Christina, it's not too late if you choose to reconsider. We could . . ."

"No, Mother," I broke in, "I have made my choice. The farther we advance, the closer Richard becomes. I cannot turn back."

"I am sorry, Christina," she said, wrapping her arms around me, "but if something happens to you, I will never forgive myself."

"I will not fail," I confidently replied, "you have taught me well."

"Sleep now," she whispered, "we leave at dawn tomorrow."

The two days it took to reach Toulon seemed to drag as heavy rains impeded our progress. When we finally did reach the city, night had already fallen and I was tired of being wet and cold. I was so worn out when we reached the inn that even the uncomfortable accommodations did not keep me from slumber.

Sleep refreshed me and I woke to a chilly sunlit morning and I could not wait to set sail for Naples. I joined Madame Duchamp in the tavern where I noticed the captain and crew of the ship lounging about as if they were waiting for something.

"Shouldn't they be on the ship?" I asked bewildered.

"The captain has just announced that we may be delayed for a while, as there is no wind, but we can fix that," she replied with a wink and removed a large black feather from her pocket with five knots in it.

"Do you intend to raise a storm?" I asked surprised.

"Not a storm," she replied, "just enough wind to get us on our way." As she began undoing the knots, she whispered,

"May these knots that I untie,

Command the wind to intensify,

Gusting and blowing southward

In the name of the dark lord."

After untying only two of the knots she stopped and knowingly said, "Two should be enough, anymore could be dangerous."

It was not more than ten minutes when one of the crewmen burst into the tavern and announced, "Captain, the southerly wind has risen and we should set sail immediately!"

With that, the captain announced that anyone leaving for Naples was to board the ship right away while the wind still cooperated. Of course I knew the wind would continue to cooperate as long as the knots that were in the feather remained untied.

"Let's go," she smiled as we left the tavern and headed for the dock. The ship was much bigger than the one that had carried us to England and I hoped the waters of the Mediterranean would be calmer than those of the English Channel.

As we boarded the huge vessel, I noticed several priests were making the journey also. One of them looked over at me with a smile and said, "May God watch over us and keep our voyage safe."

"I have no need . . . ," I began before Madame Duchamp broke in with, "Thank you, Father," and hurried me to our cabin and softly said, "A ship is the worst place to make enemies; just keep your distance from the clergy."

I did as she suggested throughout our voyage and preoccupied myself with studying and marveling at the enchanting scenery along the Italian coastline. I felt rejuvenated by the warm climate of the Mediterranean and when our ship finally docked in Naples, I was anxious to experience its wonders, as we had a few days before sailing on to Greece.

As we disembarked, customs agents were waiting to ransack tourists' luggage and confiscate illegal items. "Let me handle this," Madame Duchamp suggested.

"Anything to declare?" the customs agent abruptly asked.

"Nothing," she answered handing him a small bag of coins.

A smile instantly spread across his face as his demeanor changed, "Enjoy your stay in Naples, Signora."

"What sort of contraband are we carrying?" I asked, puzzled.

"We have certain herbs and books that would be confiscated and cause our arrest. Fortunately the customs agents are easily bribed. If anyone asks, we are just tourists; tell no one of our intentions. The church has a firm grip on Italy, it's best not to arouse suspicion," she explained.

"Understood," I agreed.

We found an inn not far from the dock that offered much more agreeable accommodations than those of the French countryside, but it was not rest that I craved but rather a need for some sort of excitement. The days on board the ship had left me bored and restless and I was glad to be on dry land again, even if it was only for a few days.

The streets of Naples were very lively with tourists and locals alike swimming and sunbathing nude on the pristine shoreline. I tried not to stare, but I couldn't help it, as we did not have such sights in France.

"It's not polite to stare," Madame Duchamp snickered, "although they are quite beautiful, aren't they?"

We had been gazing at the same group of brawny Englishmen who were trying to absorb some local color, one of whom reminded me of Richard.

"Come, Christina, there is much more to Naples than naked tourists," she said taking me by the hand.

She was undoubtedly correct, for Naples was very lively and sparkled like a jewel in the warm sun. Some peasants, dressed in festive attire, had gathered on a street corner and were dancing to the ecstatic rhythm of a jingling tambourine as the crowd that had gathered around clapped and cheered.

"Don't go too far into the crowd," Madame Duchamp cautioned, "Naples is full of expert pickpockets."

We spent the day wandering the city and admiring the landscape before the sublime setting was interrupted by a procession of shirtless men parading down the street chanting and flogging themselves with short leather whips that struck their blood-spattered backs with loud cracks. The crowds of people crossed themselves and uttered prayers as they parted to let the bloody procession through.

I turned to Madame Duchamp and curiously asked, "What was their crime?"

"They've committed no crime, Christina, they're known as the Flagellants," she replied with a hint of disgust, "they believe if they purge themselves and suffer physical pain like Christ did it will bring them closer to God."

Watching them made me revel in the fact that I was a disciple of darkness and sworn to one who did not make such demands. As they passed, my eyes met those of one of the Flagellants and his features twisted into a fearful grimace as he began to beat himself harder, the black leather strips ripping and tearing his flesh.

"Come, Christina," whispered Madame Duchamp, "before we attract attention." I followed her into the crowd and away from the bloody band of zealots as we ducked into a quiet little tavern to rest and replenish ourselves.

"It's best to keep a low profile while traveling," she declared, "It was best to get away before that Flagellant could give us away."

"But how did he know who we were?" I asked, feeling uneasy.

"Some people can sense the Power in others," she explained, "they're not exactly sure what they sense, they just know it to be evil."

Evil? I had never perceived myself or my mother as evil and it was difficult to understand how someone I had never met could see us as evil.

"Not everyone understands the pleasure and advantages of the Power, Christina," she said as if she could read my thoughts, but the puzzled expression on my face must have given me away.

We lingered for a while in the tavern before returning to the inn for the night where for the first time in weeks I slept comfortably and dreamed of being reunited with Richard. I woke in the middle of the night as I stretched out my arm across the bed to an empty space, but I knew it would not remain empty for long. Whatever fears I had earlier were melting away as each passing day brought me closer to Richard. The Power was strong within me and I was beginning to feel I could use it to overcome any obstacle that stood in my way.

I clutched the onyx stone that still adorned my neck and drifted back to sleep while thoughts of Richard's warm lips and gentle caresses filled my dreams.

"Christina, wake up, we have much to see today!" Madame Duchamp exclaimed, waking me from a sound sleep.

"It's much too early," I sleepily whined, rubbing the sleep from my eyes.

"Nonsense," she shot back, "I will meet you in the tavern."

I slowly rose and prepared myself for whatever she had in store for us, although I thought we had seen everything in Naples. As I entered the tavern, the smell of food and the sound of conversation began to awaken me.

"So what is left to see that you have awakened me so early for?" I curiously asked.

"Something extraordinary," she replied, "I promise it will be worth getting up early for."

We traveled by carriage along a dirt road until we came upon ancient ruins and what I perceived to be tunnels.

"What is this place?" I asked, gazing at the ruins that were better preserved than any I had seen so far.

"This city was buried in ancient times by an eruption, the ash and pumice covered and preserved everything," she explained.

I climbed out of the carriage in amazement as the morning sun spilled over the ruined city, casting ominous shadows down its deserted streets. We walked along the street of tombs where the city's elite rested in finely carved crypts of stone and marble.

"Much more has been unearthed since I was here," Madame Duchamp observed, glancing at the remains of what was once a sacred temple. Something about the temple seemed familiar to me as I walked toward it. The roof had long since caved in, but it was still an impressive sight and as I climbed the stone steps, I thought I detected a faint smell of incense. I stood in the middle of the ruined temple, eyes closed, haunted by a vision that was just beyond my sight.

"Christina," I felt Madame Duchamp's hand on my shoulder.

"This place seems . . . familiar to me," I whispered.

"Perhaps," she replied, "there are other lives beside this one and sometimes certain places offer us a glimpse of the past."

"A glimpse of the past," I echoed.

"Come," she smiled, "there is much more to see."

As we wandered the ancient streets, I tried to imagine what they were like in antiquity with horse-drawn carts rumbling over the cobblestones and the glint of bronze statues in the morning sunlight. Now the streets were lined with tourists arriving in carriages to explore and sketch the ruins of what must have been quite a city in its day. Most of the city was still being excavated and treasures were being hoisted to the surface from deep underground for display in museums and palaces of the nobility throughout Europe.

We followed a band of tourists descending into the tunnels to view the preserved houses of the ancient aristocracy. I carried a lantern that illuminated galleries where houses and streets remained frozen in time and in pristine condition. As my eyes adjusted to the dim light, I could detect shapes and colors on vibrantly painted walls that stood under the earth for centuries.

Intricately laid mosaics lined the floors of some of the houses, while in other houses they had been carelessly removed leaving bare stone and broken bits of tile. The paintings that still remained on the brightly colored walls looked as fresh as the day they were painted and even in the flickering light from the lantern their ancient faces stared defiantly into the face of time. Some statues of once mighty gods still lay half buried in the thick ash and pumice, but would soon be hacked out of their subterranean tombs by trea-sure seekers and once again their bronze eyes would behold the light of day.

The whole experience fascinated me and I wished to stay longer but the air in the tunnels was becoming thick and stagnant. As we ap-proached the surface, the bright sunlight was blinding and my eyes need-ed several minutes to adjust, but the air was warm and refreshing and I breathed deeply, letting it cleanse my lungs of the stale air from below. We lingered until dusk and boarded a carriage back to Naples. As we left the city behind, I watched the sun sink into the horizon, darkening the streets of the city and summoning apparitions from its romantic past. I was lost in these dreams, if dreams they were, when the carriage came to an abrupt halt that jolted me back to the present.

"Driver, why have we stopped?" Madame Duchamp asked as she poked her head out of the carriage window, only to be met with a pistol and the reply of, "Your money, Signora."

Highwaymen – so far we had been lucky enough to avoid them, and this one traveled alone, but Madame Duchamp seemed not to be frightened, but rather angry at the intrusion. She opened the door of the carriage and stepped out rather meekly, but underneath I knew she was seething.

"We haven't much, you would do well to stop the next carriage," she suggested, but the bandit rudely persisted.

"People who have very little don't ride in fine carriages such as this. Now don't waste any more of my time... your money, Signora."

As she stared hard at the thief, I noticed some vines lying in the grass began to snake their way toward the vagrant. In an instant they began to coil themselves around his legs and up to his neck causing him to drop the pistol and clutch at the strangling vines. Madame Duchamp directed her stare up the trunk of an aged tree as the vines followed her command, lynching the highwayman from one of the thick branches protruding from its ancient trunk. He kicked and gasped to no avail as the vines tightened their grip, leaving his eyes red and bulging and his body lifeless. At that moment, I saw a bright flash of light bolt from the figure suspended from the branch to Madame Duchamp on the ground below, making her Power even stronger.

"I'm sorry, Christina, I should have let you take him," she said breathlessly as she approached the carriage.

"There was no time," I assured, "I would not have acted so quickly and he would have killed us both."

"You must take notice of things around you," she instructed, "and always use whatever resources you can."

She then looked up at our astonished driver and commanded, "Tell no one what you have seen!"

"I will say nothing," he nervously stammered as he crossed himself and sped us off to Naples.

As we reached the inn, the driver seemed anxious to be rid of us as he crossed himself once again and sped off.

"Do you think he will tell anyone?" I asked.

"No matter if he does," she replied, "we will be gone in the morning anyway."

I awoke to a sun-drenched morning with a gentle breeze that would push us on toward Greece, our final stop before reaching Egypt. With each passing day I grew more anxious and restless, Naples had been a pleasant diversion, but I wanted to get to Egypt with no further delays.

"We will be in Greece for only one night before continuing on to Egypt," Madame Duchamp informed me as we boarded the ship.

She had sensed my restlessness and impatience since our journey began and did her best to make the most of our travel time.

On board the ship there was not much to do except study and prepare for what lay ahead of me. I went over things so much that I was to the point where I could recite incantations in my sleep. I read Ra-Khamin's book cover to cover and could recite passages verbatim without having to refer to the book at all. The more knowledge I gained, the more eager I was to utilize it, but the days passed very slowly and the nights even slower.

I was unable to sleep and was up on the main deck the night we reached Greece. It was a clear moonlit night and all was still on the shore, the only sound being the dark waters lapping against the ship. A warm breeze fluttered through my hair bringing the sweet smell of incense from far off in the distance. I inhaled deeply, inviting the warm air and serenity of the night to become one with me and I felt all my anxiety and tension flow out of me, leaving me with a feeling of tranquility that I had not felt in a long time. I felt relaxed enough to return to my cabin and rest comfortably in the feeling I had just experienced.

Madame Duchamp woke me early and announced, "We leave for Egypt tonight, we have the day to explore the town."

I thought about telling her about the previous night, but I decided to keep it to myself as a personal memento, so far all of my memorable events on the journey were with Madame Duchamp and although I treasured my time with her, I felt content that I had one experience that was truly my own.

As we went ashore and walked around, I was not at all impressed with the small fishing village but rather what lay outside the boundaries of the village. Ruins held a new fascination for me ever since I first caught a glimpse of them on the Italian coastline and explored the buried city outside of Naples. We wandered outside of the village in the warm sun through the olive groves and rocky hills toward the toppled columns of a once mighty temple. Madame Duchamp indulged me as I spent the better part of the day wandering among them, climbing their blackened marble steps and imagining what sort of ceremonies went on in their hallowed halls. I wished to stay longer, but Madame Duchamp reminded me of our business in Egypt.

"There are *plenty* of ruins in Egypt that you can explore when our business is done with," she promised, "I thought you were anxious for our arrival in Egypt."

"I am." I replied, somewhat embarrassed, "I just seem to lose myself in places like this."

We made our way back to the ship with little time to spare and as we left I stared longingly at the coastline and hoped to carry that serene feeling with me all the way to Egypt, but as the days passed, serenity gave way to anxiety as the boredom and restlessness returned. The days wore on into sleepless nights as I paced the deck like a caged animal . . . waiting, how I hated the waiting! I never realized how far away Egypt was and my impatience had made it even farther.

I had become irritable with a quick temper and a sharp tongue, which Madame Duchamp was quick to point out, "Christina, I have had enough of your impatience! I have tried to be understanding and comforting, but you are behaving like a spoiled brat and I will not have it!"

She would not have it? I felt my anger rise as I defiantly shot back, "You have no right to dictate my feelings, they are mine alone and I will release them however I see fit!"

"Not toward me you won't!" she snarled as I turned to leave the cabin, but she grabbed my wrist and held tight causing me to wince. "You will show me the respect I deserve and keep that anger of yours in check!"

That was the first time she had ever physically hurt me and my wounded pride answered with the Power forcing her to release me and stumble to the floor.

"You dare to raise your Power against *me*?!" she furiously ranted as she quickly regained her stance and slapped me hard across the face causing me to stumble. "Do you appreciate nothing I have done for you?!" she shouted through stinging tears, "Everything I have given you, everything I have sacrificed for you, does it all mean nothing to you?!"

I had never before seen such pain and betrayal in her eyes as I had seen at that moment and I began to tremble, *what had I done*?!

Before I could offer any explanation or apology, she softly muttered, "Get out, I can't even look at you now."

"Mother," I swallowed hard, "I . . ."

"Get out," she repeated.

I left her in the cabin, my face still stinging from the much-deserved slap she had given me. How could I have used the Power against her? She, who had placed the world at my feet and given me the key to unlock its secrets! I wandered the deck of the ship, still in shock over what I had just done until night had fallen and the rest of the passengers were in their cabins. I peered over the side of the ship down into the dark sea and thought of plunging into it, letting the dark water engulf me, forever extinguishing my fiery rage. However, I had not the courage to follow through and instead found a deserted spot on the main deck and just sat and cried under the pale moonlight; no one to hold me, no one to tell me everything would be all right.

Dawn's first light found me the next morning, my face still wet with tears and my body still shaking from shame and fear. I needed to go to her, no matter what the consequence, I needed to atone for my vile cruelty.

I softly knocked at the cabin door with trembling hand and nervously uttered, "Mother, can I come in?"

"Enter," her low tone wafted through the door.

"Mother, . . . I," my tears began to flow uncontrollably and the last thing I remembered was collapsing to the floor.

I woke several hours later, Madame Duchamp at my bedside.

"You fainted. You're feverish and exhausted."

"I am so sorry," I sobbed, "I never meant to hurt or betray you. I just couldn't *stop* myself."

"Christina, I have warned you before about controlling that temper of yours," she sadly reminded me, "I am afraid of what will happen to you if you don't."

"I swear I will *never* again direct my anger toward you," I cried.

"Maybe it's my fault. Maybe I have given you too much too soon," she confessed.

"Then take it from me," I volunteered, "I would rather have no Power than have your faith and trust in me destroyed. What I did was vile and cowardly, I don't deserve such Power."

"That's the easy way out, Christina, you know now what your anger is capable of doing and that you need to control it."

"What if I can't?" I asked with quivering voice.

"You can," she answered, "knowing that what you did was irresponsible and reckless is the first step and you can go the rest of the way."

"Will you be there with me?" I nervously asked, expecting her to tell me that I was on my own after my reprehensible behavior and she would have been justified in doing so, but instead she embraced me and whispered, "Of course I will, rest now."

"I can't," I sobbed as I set up on the edge of the bed with my head in my hands, "I know what has to be done and I am anxious to do it."

"I know, Christina," she said, wrapping her arms around my shoulders, "but there is nothing we can do until we get to Egypt. Rest now, save your energy for Abaddon."

I lay back down on the bed, but I could not relax, as every muscle was tense with anxiety.

Madame Duchamp placed her hand on my forehead and whispered, "Let it go, Christina, relax."

I closed my eyes and took a deep breath as my tension began to dissipate and my body finally felt at ease while sleep took me deep into its lair and held me in merciful captivity.

I woke the next day more refreshed than I had been since we left Greece.

"Are you well rested?" Madame Duchamp pleasantly asked.

"Yes," I replied, stretching. "Whatever you did has returned my strength."

"It's all in how you direct the Power," she replied, "something you must learn to do."

"I am most eager to learn," I offered, still feeling ashamed of what I had done and I would do everything I could to atone for it.

"We will be in Egypt the day after tomorrow, you should refresh your memory," she said, handing me the pile of books I had all but memorized, but I took them from her without protest and did as she suggested. "The more you read, the quicker the time will pass," she declared.

Although Egypt was only two days away, the time still seemed to drag no matter how much I read, but I somehow managed to keep the anxiety at bay until the night before our arrival.

"Can you make me sleep?" I desperately asked Madame Duchamp.

"You can make yourself sleep," she replied, "use your Power."

"How?" I inquired.

"The Power is not always directed outward," she explained, "Lie down, close your eyes and direct your Power *inward*." I did as she suggested and tried to relax. "Now just chant to yourself,

Sleep, Christina, sleep,

Slumber long and deep,

Safe in the Master's keep,

Sleep, Christina, sleep.'"

I began to silently chant to myself while trying to turn the Power inward.

"Think of nothing else," she whispered.

It took a while, but the more I focused on the words and thought back to the tranquil feeling I experienced in Greece, the easier it became. I could feel the tension ebb and my muscles relax before sleep took me.

"Christina! Christina!" I could hear Madame Duchamp call to me but I did not wish to leave the deep slumber that engulfed me. "Christina, please wake up!" she tearfully exclaimed as I tried to rouse myself from my sleepy prison, but try as I might . . . I could not wake.

Madame Duchamp was now shaking me, frantically trying to wake me. Since it had been the Power that had put me into such a deep slumber, I resolved to use it to draw myself out. I summoned all of my Power and shouted to myself, "WAKE!" and I was suddenly jolted awake, my heartbeat racing.

"I thought I had lost you to your own spell," Madame Duchamp said, relieved.

"I had to summon all of my Power to wake up," I confessed.

"You cast too strong a spell, you must be more careful," she warned.

"Are we in Egypt?" I asked, changing the subject.

"We are nearing Alexandria now," she smiled.

At last! All the weeks of waiting were finally over and soon I would be reunited with Richard.

We stood on the deck as the ship sailed into Alexandria. The port was very busy as other ships were docking and being relieved of cargo and passengers. As we left our ship, there were so many sights to see, I couldn't figure out where to look first.

Porters, colorfully robed and turbaned, waited impatiently for tourists, vying for their business and promising to take them to the best hotels in Alexandria. It was one of these porters, a man named Amir, who approached us and offered his services as a porter and a knowledgeable guide.

"We do not require a guide," Madame Duchamp explained, "but we do need to charter a boat to Cairo."

"I will charter a ferry for you right away, Madame," he eagerly replied as she dropped two coins into his grateful hand.

We followed him as he approached a small dock where boats called feluccas transported tourists and merchants along the ancient Nile to Cairo and beyond.

After haggling in Arabic with some of the captains, he turned to us and proudly announced, "I have negotiated a fair price for you; however, the next ferry does not leave for another hour."

"That will be fine," she replied, "thank you, Amir."

We paid for our passage to Cairo and stayed close to the port for the remaining hour. Merchants of every nationality sailed into the port of Alexandria to sell, buy or trade everything imaginable . . . even slaves. Young girls had been brought from all over Egypt and other countries of the Far East to be bought and sold in the slave market. They looked to be my age or younger with a powerful sadness in their teary eyes as they stood half naked waiting to be sold to the highest bidder.

I stopped in front of them, my eyes reflecting their sadness and revealing my own vulnerability as Madame Duchamp whispered, "Come, Christina."

"But how can they be sold like animals?" I sadly asked as she led me away. I wanted to pass my Power to every one of those girls so they may escape the bonds of their slavery and live as they wished. "Mother, can't we . . ."

"Christina, don't get involved in things that don't concern you," she answered, "Egypt is a foreign land with strange customs and we need to keep a low profile."

"But they are my age, some younger," I protested.

"This is a very poor country," she explained, "they may fare better where they are going."

"But to have no will of your own?"

"Everyone has a destiny, Christina, and yours is not to abolish slavery in foreign lands," she affirmed.

I tried to take some comfort in the fact that maybe they would have a better life than the one they would have had in a poor village, but I still could not escape the image of the misery carried in their somber eyes.

The hour passed quickly and we soon found ourselves aboard a small felucca bound for Cairo. The glass-like waters of the Nile opened up before us like a friendly hostess welcoming her guests as ruins of temples erected to forgotten gods cast eerie reflections on the placid waters. Small villages dotted the banks of the Nile, filled with people living the same as they had for thousands of years – simple farmers with no luxuries, in homes built of mud brick. Time and progress have forgotten rural Egypt, but its inhabitants didn't seem to mind at all.

The few days we spent on the Nile were pleasurable as I enjoyed the sights of ruins and desert scenery, but I could feel the anxiety growing within me.

As much as I tried to hide it, Madame Duchamp saw right through me, "I know it's hard for you, but the waiting is just about over."

"I just want the whole thing over and Richard by my side," I confessed.

"Don't' rush through this, Christina," she cautioned, "you need to take your time and keep your wits about you, don't let your anxiety make you careless."

We approached Cairo at nightfall, the lights of the city reflecting on the waters of the Nile. Although the sky was growing dark, I could see tall minarets towering over the city, stretching up toward a well-positioned crescent moon in the jeweled sky. The city seemed quite impressive and I resolved to explore it . . . with Richard by my side.

We checked into a hotel run by a Frenchman named Loiseau who assured us, "You will not find a better hotel in Cairo, we have all the comforts of Europe right here."

Indeed, he was right, the comforts in the hotel surpassed those of the French countryside that we endured as we started our journey. The first thing I did was have a long soak in the huge tub to relax and ease my tension away.

Madame Duchamp appeared in front of me, refreshed and elegantly dressed. "Have you need of sleep?"

"No," I curiously replied, "I am relaxed, but not at all tired."

"Good," she smiled, "get dressed, we are going out."

She did not say where we were going, but it was always a pleasant surprise wherever we arrived. I put on some of my finest attire and joined her in the lobby of the hotel.

"You look beautiful, my daughter," she praised.

"As do you," I said, returning her compliment, "where are we off to?"

"Come," she took me by the hand, "you will see."

We walked a few blocks north of the hotel to a vivacious café with music flowing from deep inside. As we entered, I could see that the music was coming from four people sitting cross-legged on a stage – two bearded men, a young boy and a woman. The men played stringed instruments with a long neck, a rounded piece at the middle resting atop a leg which enabled the instrument to stand while the musician sat cross-legged and dragged a bow across its strings, producing very pleasing drones. The boy kept time on a drum and the woman accompanied them on a tambourine.

As we made our way to a table close to the musicians, I could feel eyes on me as I looked around and saw mostly Europeans in the café.

"They come here for Egyptian entertainment," Madame Duchamp said, noticing my observation.

"Have you been to this place before?" I asked.

"Many times," she replied, as the musicians finished their song to thunderous applause. They smiled at the crowd as they began their next tune, this one being more up-tempo and lively. As the music began to swell, two women dressed in brightly colored silks emerged from backstage and began to perform a slow yet rhythmic dance as they whirled with the pleasant chimes from their finger cymbals perfectly complimenting the music. The musicians picked up their tempo, provoking the dancers to quicken their steps. Faster and faster to the swelling music they moved, entranced by the sounds of the instruments and the pure joy of dance until they became gyrating rainbows of silks. The audience began to clap along to the music providing a more frenzied atmosphere as music and the dance rose to a fever pitch, creating an aura of sensual ecstasy. The energy in the whole room was electrifying as audience, dancers and musicians became one for a fleeting moment, as lovers entwined, before the music wound up in an intense crescendo that left all involved in passionate rapture.

I had been so engrossed in what was going on, I did not even notice that food and drink had been placed on our table. I didn't feel the least bit hungry, but took advantage of the generous supply of champagne.

"Are you enjoying yourself?" Madame Duchamp asked over the tumultuous applause.

"Very much," I replied, "it was . . . magical."

She then motioned to one of the waiters who promptly responded, "What can I get for you, Madame?"

"Will you please tell Rakesh El-Khaliq that Madame Duchamp wishes to see him?"

"At once," he replied.

"He owns this place," she explained, "and had taught me much when I was seeking knowledge of the Black Arts."

A tall, bearded man wearing a turban quickly approached our table, "Madeline, is that really you?"

"It is, old friend," she replied, rising to embrace him.

"And who is this beautiful maiden by your side?" he eloquently asked.

"My daughter, Christina Lafage," she proudly announced.

"It is a pleasure, Monsieur," I responded, "the entertainment you have here is spectacular."

"Thank you, my young friend," he humbly replied, "and may I say you have your mother's beauty."

"You are very kind, Rakesh," Madame Duchamp warmly stated, "Won't you join us?"

"I would be honored," he graciously accepted.

"What brings you to Egypt?" he asked.

"Christina is on the left hand path. I have passed all of my knowledge on to her. She is my legacy," she proudly stated, "but she insists on journeying to the land of the dead to reclaim her slain lover."

"That is a very dangerous undertaking for one so young," he warned.

"I am prepared to face whatever danger lies ahead and return un-scathed," I assured.

He turned to Madame Duchamp and mused, "Your daughter has your determination. What of your Power, Christina? Do you feel it strong enough?"

"I have taken lives and felt my Power grow stronger, coursing through my veins like lightning," I answered, "But I have let emotion interfere and take control of the Power."

"Her Power is very strong," Madame Duchamp offered, "but I still do not wish for her to go through with this, I cannot dissuade her."

"I could not dissuade you either as I remember," he said to her, "you went for money, Christina goes for love. The reasons are different but the risk is the same. You have told her of the risk?"

"I have told her everything, but she still insists on making the jour-ney," she replied, "She has studied the incantations and has read the Book of the Dead as well as Ra-Khamin's book."

"Your mother cares for you a great deal," he said to me.

"I know," I replied, "and there is nothing I would refuse her, but I have to do this."

He looked at me for a few moments and then turned to Madame Duchamp, "You have instructed and prepared her?"

"I have," she answered.

He proceeded to test my knowledge on everything from herbs to pas-sages from Ra-Khamin's book; he tested me for hours, but there was nothing he asked that I could not answer.

"You have instructed her well," he said, "I am most impressed."

"Thank you, Rakesh, your opinion means a great deal to me," she humbly replied.

"Christina, if you feel you are ready, then I will help you," he firmly stated, "In two nights there will be no moon, that is when you must go."

"Thank you, Rakesh, I will follow whatever instructions you give me without failure," I assured.

"Excellent," he smiled, "now, where are you staying?"

"There is a hotel a few blocks from here run by a Frenchman . . ." Madame Duchamp began before Rakesh broke in, "You will stay with me."

"That is very kind, old friend," she answered, "but we could not impose."

"It is no imposition," he affirmed, "I would be honored to have you as my guests."

"Well," she smiled, "your guests we shall be."

"I will have your things brought to my home at once," he said as he motioned to one of the servants and gave him instructions in Arabic.

We enjoyed the rest of the evening in Rakesh's company with free-flowing champagne and superb entertainment. It was very late when the café closed and we walked the two blocks to Rakesh's house, or palace would have been a better description. The house was huge with many rooms and just as many servants. The room I was led to had elaborately painted columns and ancient Egyptian scenery adorned the walls. A large west-facing balcony overlooked the lights of the city with the Nile and the western desert beyond in the distance.

Although the view was breathtakingly beautiful, the need for sleep took precedence as I climbed into bed and sailed down the stream of sleep.

I awoke to the morning sun pouring into the room through the open balcony. The warmth of the sun drew me toward the balcony as I looked on the bustling city below. As I stood absorbing the sun's heat, I heard a commanding, yet passionate, voice singing in low and mournful tones. I could not understand the words, but it did not seem to matter. It was the sheer beauty of the different tones of the voice that had captivated me and just as quickly as it had started, it abruptly ceased. I listened for a few moments, hoping it would return, but my vigil was not rewarded.

I dressed and joined Madame Duchamp in the great banquet hall where Rakesh joined us moments later. I told him about the voice I had heard and asked if he knew where it came from.

"What you heard was the Muslim call to prayer," he explained, "there are several mosques in Cairo and Muslim prayers are said throughout the day, you will hear it again."

We spent most of the day in the Cairo marketplace – where most Egyptians spent most of their time buying food for the night's banquet, haggling over prices or meeting in social groups. The marketplace was cluttered with goods and crowds of people haggling for the best price. Colorful silk fabrics hung like a rainbow in the booth of one merchant who was arguing with the silk merchant next to him in increasingly loud tones.

"They are arguing over who has the better merchandise," Rakesh laughed.

Camels, overloaded with goods were being pulled along by their masters who would sell the goods and even the camel for the right price while the smells from the spice market wafted through the air. A jewelry merchant motioned for me to approach him, and out of curiosity I went over to his small booth followed by Madame Duchamp and Rakesh. He said something to me in Arabic and pointed to the onyx stone that adorned my neck.

"He wants to buy your necklace," Rakesh translated, "he says he will give you a fair price."

"Tell him I cannot part with this for any price," I solemnly replied as I ran my fingers over the cool stone.

"A gift from your lover?" he asked.

"Yes," I said, "Richard gave this to me the night before he was taken from me."

Rakesh explained to the merchant and the merchant nodded and smiled as we moved along through the marketplace.

Baskets of fruit, bottles of perfume, incense, tea, carpets – there was nothing the marketplace did not have. When we were through, I had two bottles of perfume and a small pouch of incense, while Madame Duchamp had purchased some rare herbs.

It was after the marketplace that I was introduced to the dreary side of Cairo. Madame Duchamp had told me that Egypt was a poor country, but I had no idea how poor.

Beggars lined the streets, stretching out thin, weakened arms asking for a few coins with a look of hopelessness in their eyes. Poverty did not seem to discriminate. Men, women and children were all in need of financial aid. I had seen poverty in France, but not to this extent. At least France had poorhouses, here there was nothing; people lived in the sandy streets while children played in the shadow of hanged criminals in the town square.

"So now you have seen something of the world and how ruthless it can be," Madame Duchamp whispered to me.

"Yes," I replied, relieved that the path had kept me out of poverty. But besides being ruthless, the world could also hold much beauty as the Muslim call to prayer reminded me, as once again its voice floated on the warm wind toward my grateful ears. The sound was coming from a nearby mosque with tall, ornately carved minarets and domes topped with a metal crescent moon that gleamed in the late afternoon sun. The entrance was very ornamental with floral designs and lattice patterns that fell like lace over windows and balconies.

I walked toward the entrance, but felt something pull me back, "No, Christina," Rakesh whispered, "Women are not allowed in the mosque."

"No women at all?" I curiously asked.

"No women," he replied.

That was the first time something had been denied to me since acquiring the Power, I thought there was nothing I could not have or do.

"Please do not be offended," Rakesh apologized, "but it is Muslim law."

"The role of women is very different here," Madame Duchamp explained, "they don't enjoy the same freedoms as European women."

I had noticed the women in the marketplace – veiled from head to foot with only a small opening for the eyes. I thought them very mysterious and perhaps members of some sort of cult, but Rakesh explained that also was part of Muslim law.

Rakesh took us to the outskirts of the city to a ruined temple where mammoth statues of a forgotten pharaoh stood buried knee-deep in the unforgiving sand. As we walked past them toward the temple entrance, I noticed the regal face of the king with his painted eyes and royal beard.

Arms of stone crossed his mighty chest holding the crook and flail – great symbols of power to the ancients.

The inside of the temple was lit by torches, as even the sun dared not to enter this sacred place. We ventured farther into the temple to a small room supported by vast columns, most of which still held their original paint.

Two men, whom I remembered as the musicians from Rakesh's café, sat on cushions around a strange-looking apparatus with long tubes connected to it and a sweet smell emanating from the top. Rakesh greeted the men and instructed us to be seated on the cushions surrounding what I was told was a "hookah."

"The day has been long and we have much ahead of us tomorrow," Rakesh announced, "so let us enjoy some leisure."

The hookah seemed to be in four pieces – a body partly filled with water, a small cup on top of the body containing tiny brown balls, long tubes connected to the middle of the body and mouthpieces of amber connected to each tube.

"What is it?" I asked Madame Duchamp as she handed me one of the tubes.

"Opium," she answered, "it will relax you. You smoke it, like this."

I watched her demonstrate as she placed the amber mouthpiece between her lips and inhaled deeply, causing the water in the hookah to bubble, producing a very pleasing sound. As she removed the mouthpiece, she closed her eyes for a few seconds before releasing the smoke into the sweetly scented air

"Try it?" she asked, handing me one of the tubes with the smooth amber mouthpiece.

I did as she demonstrated, inhaling deep as sweet tasting smoke filled my mouth and flowed deep into my lungs and as I exhaled I did acquire a feeling of serenity.

"It has quite a sweet taste," I said to her before drawing more from the bubbling hookah.

"The pomegranate juice in the water gives it the sweet flavor," she explained.

Rakesh's musicians put down their tubes, picked up their instruments and began playing soothing, melodious tunes that seemed to intensify my serene feeling. The more I smoked, the more intense the music became and the more aware I felt. I looked around at the temple and noticed the paintings that adorned the stone walls. How vivid and rich the color was! Even in the torchlight, they seemed so. . . . alive! Paintings of pharaohs bearing offerings to animal-headed gods were once again alive as I rose to my feet to see them more closely. My whole body was propelled into a state of euphoria as the music swirled around me and I could swear I could actually *see* the music. The music had also affected the wall paintings, as they were no longer paintings but actual beings performing mysterious rituals once again in their hallowed sanctuary.

My eyes rose to the ceiling where I beheld a vault of stars as a winged goddess stretched her brightly colored feathers across the night sky sheltering all beneath her. Boats sailed once again on swift currents as the gods of ancient Egypt came once again to dance and allowed me to bear witness to it.

I felt as though I had consumed vats of wine but had none of the clumsiness associated with alcohol, my senses were not dulled but *sharpened* as everything around me teemed with life and color.

"Christina, come," Madame Duchamp whispered, "we must go."

I did not wish to leave, but when I turned to her to protest, her eyes displayed a deep blue wildness that made me want to follow her.

"Come," she smiled as I took her hand and thanked the ancients for allowing me passage into their mysterious land. The warmth of the desert permeated my entire being, drawing me out of the temple and into its embrace. Night had fallen, but despite the absence of the moon, I could see color everywhere. Rakesh led the way with a torch that seemed to me like the sun itself was burning brightly atop his torch, illuminating the entire city of Cairo. As we walked the streets, brightly colored tents fluttered in the gentle breeze as light blared from houses and mosques.

"How different everything looks!" I shouted to Madame Duchamp above the music that only I could hear. I was sure it was music – the gentle breezes, the footfalls of a passerby, the baying of dogs – it was all music to me.

When we returned to Rakesh's house, I stood on the balcony looking down at the sea of lights before me. They flickered and danced in every color imaginable before my wondrous eyes and I could not turn away from the dazzling display.

"Christina, how do you feel?" Madame Duchamp asked as she entered the room.

"Extraordinary," I smiled as I gazed into the electric blue of her eyes.

"We have much to do tomorrow, my daughter," she warmly said, stroking my hair, "it is late and you should rest."

Rest? How could I rest when I felt so alive and my senses so aware?

"I cannot rest now," I told her, "I have never before seen the world this way."

"The feeling is temporary, you will feel tired soon and sleep will come," she softly said, "I will stay here with you."

Soon, later – I had no concept of time; it did not seem to matter. My only desire was to stare out at the sea of lights that was Cairo. As I looked down into the lights, a familiar face looked up at me and I leapt from the balcony into the glaring lights below. My body felt weightless as I floated down into the soft sand where Richard stood, as warm and alive as I remembered him.

"Come to me, Christina, I've waited so long," he whispered as he held his arms out toward me.

I anxiously ran toward him, but my footsteps became heavy and it seemed like an eternity before I reached him, but just before my hands touched him he was gone and I was stretched out on the bed as dawn began to break. I didn't remember falling asleep, but my dream of Richard was emblazoned on my memory and my urge to confront Abaddon and bargain for Richard burned inside me stronger than ever.

I stood on the balcony watching the city come to life, keeping my thoughts focused on the task ahead of me.

"Christina?" Madame Duchamp quietly knocked on the door and I bade her enter. "How do you feel this morning, daughter? It was quite a while before you fell asleep."

"Invigorated and ready for the journey," I confidently answered.

"Are you sure?" she nervously asked.

"Yes, even now I feel my Power stirring within me, driving me," I answered.

"I see a look of determination in your eyes I've not seen before," she declared.

"I dreamed of Richard," I confessed, "He was as I remembered him, but just beyond my reach. Tonight will be no dream and he will not be beyond my grasp."

"Then let us prepare for this evening," she said, taking me by the hand.

8

I was given a bath in water drawn from the Nile with the herbs Madame Duchamp had purchased the previous day added to the warm water. She chanted incantations I had recognized from Ra-Khamin's book as well as those from <u>The Book of the Dead.</u> My body was then sprinkled with sweet-smelling oils and draped in fine linen.

"Abaddon will find you most appealing, use your charms to your advantage," she advised.

We met Rakesh in his huge library where an open copy of Ra-Khamin's <u>Descent Into Nekyia</u> lay on the desk where Rakesh sat.

"We are ready, Rakesh," Madame Duchamp announced.

"You know what to expect, my young friend?" he inquired as he rose from behind the desk.

"I am ready and more than willing," I replied.

I felt strangely at ease, yet determined as my anxiety and fear had melted away. I wondered if the opium from the night before had been a contributing factor; it had certainly made my senses aware, but did my courage and determination come from the drug or did it spring from deep inside me? Had I finally come of age and left the frightened child behind? The night's task that lay before me would surely answer my questions and put my Power and knowledge to the ultimate test.

The three of us walked through the crowded streets to the muddy banks of the Nile where we boarded a small felucca.

"Where are we sailing to?" I asked Rakesh.

"Down the Nile and across to the western desert," he replied, "There, just beyond the pyramids lies the Temple of Set."

As we sailed the calm waters of the Nile under the warm Egyptian sun, my thoughts drifted back to the paintings I had seen on the walls of the opium-filled temple of barges sailing down the Nile carrying the pharaoh's body to its final resting place. The only difference was this was not a funeral barge, but one of resurrection.

When we reached the village of Giza, the majestic pyramids loomed in the distance and I marveled at their size and beauty. Rakesh had procured camels, one for each of us and a fourth laden with supplies to take us to our destination that lay just beyond the pyramids.

"We will have to camp in the desert tonight," Rakesh explained, "it is perilous to cross the desert on a night with no moonlight."

The idea of camping in the desert did not at all appeal to me, but I would endure anything to have Richard by my side.

As we crossed the desert, the pyramids grew even larger and I saw a large stone head towering above the sand.

"The Sphinx," Madame Duchamp said, pointing to the huge head, "it has watched the sun rise over this desert for thousands of years."

"The Arabs call it Abu el-Hol," Rakesh added, "Father of Terror."

It did not look frightening to me at all, but rather mysterious and clever, as if it was privy to knowledge long forgotten by humanity. It wore the headdress of a pharaoh and despite its missing nose, had a most regal appearance. The eyes and headdress still bore traces of their original color that must have been as vivid in ancient times as they were in my opium dreams.

A caravan was camped beneath the great statue selling pottery and trinkets to tourists who had stopped to rest their camels and sketch the Sphinx to accompany their stories to friends and relatives back home. Although I desperately wanted to stop and explore the Sphinx more closely, I knew that we did not have time for such things, as night would soon befall us and my journey needed to take precedence. I silently bid the Sphinx farewell as we continued toward the massive pyramids. It seemed as if they rose to the sun itself as they cast long shadows on the sand below.

I stared at them in amazement as Rakesh said, "They are quite impressive, are they not?"

"I have never seen anything so immense," I answered, "the largest building I have seen before embarking on this journey was Notre Dame."

"Many Notre Dames would fit inside the Great Pyramid," he smiled.

Crowds of tourists swarmed around the Great Pyramid; many were trying to climb to its dizzying heights while others searched for artifacts.

We rode for miles past the pyramids where no tourists ventured and I began to wonder where the Temple of Set was, since I could see nothing but desert before us. Rakesh had finally stopped and helped us dismount, but there was nothing but mounds of sand and the hot sun above. I was just about to ask Madame Duchamp why we had stopped, when Rakesh raised his arms to the sky and began to chant in Arabic as I felt my Power strongly circulating through me. As Rakesh continued his chant, I noticed the sand covering a large mound begin to recede, revealing the ruins of a small temple. The columns were all toppled – not one of them stood, and the temple just seemed to be a pile of debris. We walked among the toppled columns to what appeared to be a stone altar stained with centuries of blood. As Rakesh raised his hands the stone altar slid back, revealing steps carved into solid rock.

"An underground temple?" I excitedly asked Rakesh.

"Centuries ago, worship of Set was outlawed and his followers were forced underground, where we have remained," he explained as we descended into the subterranean depths.

I was given a torch that I was able to light with a wave of my hand and received a wink of approval from Madame Duchamp. We descended deep into the earth until we reached the Temple of Set. Huge elaborately carved columns supported the ceiling of earth and as more torches were lit, I was a bit taken aback by the artwork that decorated the walls. The god, Set, was depicted on the walls of his temple accepting sacrifices from his disciples and bestowing Power and favors upon them. The god was dressed in royal Egyptian headdress and kilt, but despite his Egyptian attire and name, the face that looked back at me was Lucien's.

"The Master's Power stretches far and wide, Christina," Madame Duchamp whispered, noticing my surprise.

An altar, much like the one in the abandoned church where we had held the Black Mass, stood in an immense alcove surrounded by pits of bones and burnt offerings, while another alcove housed a stone tub, containing the sacred waters of the Nile. As I looked around the temple, my ears detected the distinct sound of water lapping against a shore and as we ventured farther, the temple opened up to a vast underground river and I could just see light in the distance. I sat on the rocky shore, closed my eyes and began to clear my mind. I thought of nothing except that which lay before me. I reviewed everything I had been taught as well as key passages from Ra-Khamin's Descent Into Nekyia and the Book of the Dead.

Madame Duchamp and Rakesh had been busy lighting incense and numerous candles to honor Set in his secret temple. The aroma of the incense wafted toward me and I inhaled deeply as I listened to the rhythm of the water gently washing against the shore.

I sat for some time before feeling a hand on my shoulder, indicating that it was time for the journey to begin.

"The sky above has grown dark," Rakesh informed me, "it is time to summon the ferryman."

I stood and walked over to a large statue of the god Set and spoke a key passage from The Book of the Dead as I knelt before it,

"I kneel before you, Lord Set,

And serve you without regret,

I pray, release the ferry of the dead,

To carry me to my task ahead."

I looked longingly at the statue that bore Lucien's features as the Power strongly stirred within me. I slowly rose, returned to the shore and summoned the ferryman with the words from chapter five of <u>Descent Into Nekyia</u>:

"Lord of the river, I summon you here,

By your master Set, now appear,

Grant me passage on your ancient ferry,

Along the current to Abaddon's sanctuary."

I began to see a vessel slowly approaching in the distance, gliding along the dark water.

"Remember, Christina, show Abaddon no fear. No one is invulnerable," Madame Duchamp whispered.

I nervously turned to her and said, "Mother, what if . . ."

"Follow your heart, Christina," she said, putting her finger to my lips, "Don't doubt yourself and let the Power guide you."

I felt the Power within me, but it did not calm the fear inside me. No matter what, I had to keep the fear hidden from Abaddon if I was to return to the world of the living.

"You have taught me well, I will not fail," I said to Madame Duchamp.

"Come back to me, Christina," she tearfully replied as she embraced me, "I have done all I can, you must rely on yourself now. Do what you must, just return to me."

"I will," I replied as I withdrew from her tender embrace and turned to face the approaching vessel.

"May Set watch over you," Rakesh offered as the boat reached the shore.

The boat appeared to be made of a green stone – like material with a serpent's head at the front. The ferryman was a tall, forlorn figure in a long tattered robe and a chain about his waist. He possessed two expressionless faces – one facing forward and one backward to prevent souls who have not paid the fare from boarding the moving boat.

"You do not belong to this world," he solemnly whispered, "what business have you in the world of the dead?"

"I go to bargain with Abaddon for my lover's release," I firmly stated.

He looked at me rather dispassionately and replied, "The fare will be double and paid in advance, lest you fail."

I dropped two coins into his icy hand and asserted, "Failure is an option that I do not have."

"What is your name, brave girl?" he asked.

"Christina Lafage," I answered.

"Enter, Christina Lafage," he said as he stepped back, allowing me entry into his boat.

I kept my eyes focused forward into the distant light and did not look back at the shore. I could not bear to see the tears in Madame Duchamp's eyes as we sailed away.

As we made our way down the river, I could see the light getting brighter and could see mountains on either shore with immense lakes of fire giving off the bright light.

The souls of the dead lined the shore, naked and emaciated, wailing in lament as we passed. "Look, all you damned," one of them shouted, "one of the living has come to bear witness to our torment! Do you like what you see, fair maiden?! Come, join us here on the shore, we will satisfy your curiosity!"

I ignored their taunting, keeping my thoughts focused on my task.

The river wound through a narrow gorge to a sandy shore where a well-worn path twisted into the distance.

"Follow the path to the gateway to the dead," the ferryman spoke, "there you will find Abaddon."

I thanked the ferryman as I climbed out of his boat and headed down the path. I walked the path, feeling more alone than I had ever felt; my heart beating with fear and anticipation. What would Abaddon ask of me? Would my Power be strong enough to defeat him? The questions and lingering fear swam through my mind despite my best efforts to quell them as I walked the deserted path that wound through steep crags and rocky terrain.

I wished that Madame Duchamp had been with me, her presence had always been a comfort as well as a source of knowledge, but it was time for me to rely on myself and use the knowledge I had gained from her. Hopefully, I had gained the wisdom to use the Power wisely and not let fear weaken my confidence. I clutched my onyx stone as if to draw strength from it and kept moving down the path.

The path ended at an immense gateway constructed entirely of skulls and bones of the dead. The empty eye sockets peered eerily from all directions as I made my way closer, but just before I could pass through, a figure emerged from beyond and blocked my way.

"The living are not permitted beyond the portal of the dead," it barked.

"I have come a long way," I replied, "I wish to see Abaddon."

"I am Phaeton, the gatekeeper. What business have you with Abaddon?"

"That is between myself and your master," I firmly answered.

"Leave this place, forget your business with Abaddon and return to the world of the living," he insisted.

I had not expected such opposition and my patience was wearing thin, "Summon your master, Abaddon, and tell him Christina Lafage wishes to speak with him."

"What is it you require, Christina Lafage?" a voice from behind Phaeton asked.

"Show yourself!" I commanded.

A tall being emerged from the shadows, bearded and pale he was, with long flowing hair tucked behind pointed ears. His skin was scaly, like a serpent's and covered with coarse hair. Despite his beastly appearance, he displayed a sense of sophistication that rang with an arrogance that made me uneasy, as I could not help but stare into his glowing eyes.

"I am Abaddon," he hissed, his tongue caressing sharp fangs. "Shame on you, Phaeton, for keeping such a beautiful lass waiting. What is it you wish to discuss, fair maiden?"

"Greetings, Lord Abaddon," I nervously offered, "I have come to ask you to release one who was taken before his time."

"You are here for love? I could give you love, my lady," he smoothly replied.

"I am sure you could, my lord," I politely answered, "but it is a mortal that I seek."

"I see," he smiled, "and what is this mortal's name?"

"Richard Ridgewood," I answered.

"Phaeton!" he shouted, "bring this man before me!"

"As you command," Phaeton replied and disappeared through the gateway to the forest beyond.

"You remind me of someone," he said as his glowing eyes moved up and down my body.

"I'm sure you've had the pleasures of many women, lord," I nervously complimented.

"Oh, I have. But something about you rings familiar, although you have never been here before," he pondered.

I swallowed hard and hoped that he would not connect me to Madame Duchamp, who had tricked him years earlier and barely escaped. The thought had made me even more distressed, but I desperately tried to bury the fear deep within me as Abaddon moved closer to me.

"You have fear in you, fair maiden, despite the brave front you put on," he detected, "does my presence intimidate you?"

What arrogance, but I would play along if it would help free Richard.

"Forgive me, but I am not used to being before one such as you," I lied.

Just then, Phaeton returned with Richard beside him. My heart ached, I wanted to rush toward him and throw my arms around him as I just barely stopped the tears that began to well up in my eyes. He looked so gaunt and miserable and his body still bore the bullet wounds that cut him down.

"Christina!" he cried with surprise, "Leave here, this is a place of death and misery. I do not wish to see you in such a place."

"Your lover has come for your release," Abaddon said to him, "But I cannot just let him go, Mademoiselle Lafage."

Finally the bargaining had begun; I took a deep breath and prepared myself for whatever he might ask.

"What do you ask of me, Lord Abaddon?" I firmly asked.

A wide grin spread across his face as his eyes glowed with wild excitement. "Your Power is very strong," he said as he circled around me, "I sensed it the moment you approached."

"My Power has been bestowed upon me by your master," I asserted.

"But the lives you have taken have strengthened and nurtured it," he observed, "I've not sensed such Power in a very long time."

He continued to circle me as I wondered what sort of plot he was hatching behind those glowing eyes. "Have no fear, Christina Lafage, I am not an unreasonable sort," he began, "I will let this man return to you . . . if you surrender your Power to me."

"Christina, no!" Richard exclaimed.

"Let her make the choice!" Abaddon shot back at him.

Surrender my Power? No Power would leave me weak and vulnerable . . . and unable to escape. Suddenly, everything Madame Duchamp had taught me came rushing through my brain, there must be something she taught me that would enable me to outwit him and escape with Richard.

"You ask a very high price for just one soul," I nervously uttered, trying to buy some time.

"Everything has its price, my dear," he sneered, "and my offer is not open to negotiation."

I looked longingly at Richard. I could not leave him behind, not after everything I had gone through.

"Don't do it, Christina," he cried, "I love you too much to let this foul beast deceive you."

"Enough!" Abaddon shouted, and motioned for Phaeton to restrain Richard. "Make your decision now, your Power in exchange for this mortal!"

For the first time I had tasted the bitter tang of pure fear as I looked straight into Abaddon's eyes of fire and knelt before him.

"Take it," I stammered.

"Are you sure?" he triumphantly asked.

"Christina, no!" Richard shouted.

"Do it!" I commanded.

My heart beat furiously and sweat began to run down my forehead as everything I had learned began to rapidly run through my mind. Finally, one of the last things Madame Duchamp had told me, "Use your resources," burst through as I knelt squeezing the warm sand between my fingers. That's it! As Abaddon stretched out his claw-like hand to take my power, I grabbed two heaping handfuls of sand and flung them as hard as I could into his glowing pits of fire. His ear-piercing shriek echoed throughout the underworld as I jumped to my feet and pulled Richard away from Phaeton's grasp.

"Run!" I screamed and bolted down the path with Richard's hand in mine. About halfway down the path, I stopped to look back and saw two figures in pursuit.

"Christina!" Richard shouted as I turned to him and put my finger to my lips and faced Abaddon and Phaeton.

I felt my fear melting into anger as I raised my arms above my head and shouted,

"Winds of the abyss, arise!

Save me from an untimely demise,

Carry the sand as you gust and swirl,

And a mighty storm at my pursuers hurl!"

I closed my eyes and concentrated all my Power to the command I had just shouted to the wind as I felt it blow through my hair and toward Abaddon and Phaeton. It quickly developed into a swirling black cloud of sand and as my anger toward Abaddon rose, so the sandstorm became more intense, slamming toward them, obstructing their view and making pursuit impossible. I felt the Power swirling within and around me carrying out my command in a forceful burst of energy that I had never before unleashed. The winds blew even stronger, carrying the stinging sands into a furious tempest that demanded much of my energy.

"Christina!" Richard shouted over the roaring wind, "We must go!"

I grabbed his hand and we ran down the path to the shore where the ferryman still waited in his ancient boat.

"Get in," I said to Richard as we reached the boat.

"Where does this river lead?" he asked.

"Back to me," I replied, stroking his cheek, "Once you cross this river you will be whole again."

He took me in his arms and squeezed me tightly, his embrace was cold and the smell of the grave emanated from him, but I did not care. He would live again as soon as we crossed the river.

"I love you," he whispered.

"We must leave now," the ferryman announced, "you have enraged the Lord of the Dead and it is not wise to linger here."

We climbed into the boat and began our trek along the river. The farther we got from the shore, Richard grew weaker and began to wince in pain.

"What is it?" I asked as he lay down in the boat.

"I. . .I'm beginning to *feel*."

The bullet wounds he still bore began to turn a deep red as he started to reel from the pain.

"What's happening to me?" he gasped.

"Rebirth is painful, my love," I replied as I held him close to me, feeling him slowly becoming warmer and color returning to his ashen face.

As we reached the shore where Madame Duchamp and Rakesh waited, Richard's pain grew more intense and his wounds began to bleed.

"Christina!" shouted Madame Duchamp as I emerged from the boat. "I was so worried," she cried as she took me in her arms, "The waiting was agonizing. Are you all right?"

"I am a bit weak, but my Power is still intact," I replied, "I raised a powerful storm against Abaddon and it seems to have weakened me."

"We must get him into the water," Rakesh suggested, looking down at Richard.

Rakesh helped Richard out of the boat and onto the shore where Richard was led to the stone tub filled with water from the Nile.

"This water will soothe your pain," Rakesh told him as he helped Richard into the tub.

"Thank you, mother," I cried, still in her embrace, "I would not have made it back had it not been for all of your teaching."

"I'm just relieved to have you back," she said, "I would have crossed the river and faced Abaddon's wrath myself if you did not return."

As we parted, I turned to thank the ferryman but he had already disappeared down the winding river.

I stood by the stone tub where Richard soaked in the healing water that quelled his pain. The bullet wounds were gone and as I ran my hand over his chest, I could feel his heart beating. His body was warm and filled with life once again and my Power had been responsible.

"How do you feel, Richard?" I asked as he looked up at me.

"Weak," he smiled, "but overjoyed to be with you again. Where are we?"

"This is the Temple of Set in the Egyptian desert. That man over there is Rakesh El-Khaliq, he brought us here," I answered.

"Egypt," he sounded surprised, "you came all the way to Egypt from France for me?"

"For you alone," I replied as I leaned over the stone tub and kissed his warm lips.

"You have risked much for me, Christina, I don't know how to begin to thank you," he said.

"You are worth everything I have risked," I whispered.

"How are you feeling, Richard?" Madame Duchamp asked as she and Rakesh moved toward us.

"Alive, but weak," he answered.

"The weakness will pass," she replied, "We should return to the surface, our work here is finished and Richard needs to rest."

Rakesh helped Richard up the steps of the subterranean temple as Madame Duchamp and I followed. As I passed the huge statue of Set, I knelt before it and whispered, "Thank you, Lucien."

Night had fallen on the desert above the temple and I was glad to be out of the temple and in the cool night air. A gentle breeze glided across the desert and I felt rejuvenated as it washed over me. I felt relieved that the whole ordeal was finally over and I had emerged unscathed with Richard. My Power was put to the ultimate test and I had proved myself worthy against such a formidable opponent.

"So what did Abaddon ask of you?" Madame Duchamp inquired as I stood praising my actions.

"He asked me to surrender my Power to him," I replied, "but I outwit him."

I proudly related everything that had taken place with Abaddon and triumphantly proclaimed, "I have conquered my fear and cheated death."

"You have done exceptionally well and I am proud of you, Christina, but don't become overconfident. The Power will enable you to have anything you desire if you use it wisely, but overconfidence breeds nothing but ignorance," she cautioned.

"I just feel so sure of myself now," I confessed, "and I had not felt that before."

"Walk the path with confidence, but be cautious, for there are those who will stop at nothing to seek the destruction of the Power," she warned.

"Their lives will strengthen our Power," I declared as she smiled at me and replied, "Indeed they will."

I shared a tent with Richard watching him with smoldering desire as he slept. His eyes opened and his lips called to me, warm and soft as I spread myself over him and caressed his lips with my own.

"I've ached for you, Richard," I whispered as I slid out of the loose-fitting linen garment and ran my tongue along his throat. His hands caressed my flesh, awakening the deep fire of arousal within me.

"I've longed to have you back in my arms, Christina," he softly confessed, holding me tightly and kissing me with intense passion. My body was engulfed in ecstasy as he penetrated me and I arched my back, driving him in deeper.

"Slow, Richard, slow," I seductively whispered, wanting to prolong the sensual rhythm that fed my hunger for him. I moved with the slow, steady motion of his body and the music of his breathing, further arousing my inflamed desire as beads of sweat glistened on our bodies. We savored the sweet rhythm until we could no longer hold back and climaxed in a symphony of soft tones of pleasure. The encounter had left us both worn out, but satisfied as we slept in each other's arms.

I awoke early in the morning and this time when I stretched out my arm, it met with Richard's sleeping form next to me. I softly kissed him, wrapped myself in a blanket and stepped out onto the warm sand to greet the sunrise. The morning seemed more tranquil than others and I felt more relaxed than I had ever felt. With the previous night's task behind me, I felt as if a great weight had been lifted from my shoulders and I could breathe easy. A soft desert breeze wafted toward me and I closed my eyes and tilted my head back, letting it glide over me and wash away all of the tension and angst that had plagued me since I had left France. I sensed a warm presence behind me, rising like the sun and felt its arms around my waist.

"What a beautiful morning," Richard whispered in my ear, "many times have I longed to see the sun again."

"How are you feeling this morning?" I asked, turning to face him.

"Alive," he smiled and tenderly embraced me, "Thank you, Christina."

We joined Madame Duchamp and Rakesh near the huge sand dune that concealed the Temple of Set.

"Eat something, Richard," Madame Duchamp advised, handing him a small basket of fruit, "you need to regain your strength."

"Thank you, Madame," he replied, "I do still feel a bit weak."

"That will pass and you will regain your strength and vitality," she affirmed.

Richard did look weak, now that I saw him in the daylight. He was thin and pale and I could see the outline of his ribcage beneath his tattered rags. He ate much, savoring every bite as he did.

"Forgive me," he apologized, "but it has been so long since I have tasted anything."

"Then we will prepare a feast for you tonight, young man," Rakesh announced, "with many things to satisfy your palate."

"That sounds wonderful," Richard replied as we packed up and headed back toward the Nile.

As we were on our way, I told Richard everything that had happened to me since his funeral. He listened intently as I related all of the events that had unfurled and how they had affected me, but I knew that what I had gone through was minor compared to what Richard had endured. He seemed a bit reluctant to talk about it and said that he did not remember much about what the land of the dead was like.

"I do remember being shot," he began, "I remember the pain and your tears and ceasing to breathe. I remember crossing the river and seeing Abaddon, but nothing beyond that."

"Maybe some things aren't meant to be remembered," I offered in a comforting tone.

"You were always in my thoughts, Christina. I knew that somehow I would see you again," he confessed.

As we sailed back across the Nile, I continued to inform Richard of every detail of the journey that had brought me to Egypt.

"You have achieved much, Christina," he smiled, "and have seen more in the past few months than most people see their entire lives."

"I intend to achieve even more," I confessed, "The Power has made me strong and I will continue to learn as much as I can."

"And I will be there, right beside you," he affirmed.

The small felucca reached the muddy shore of the Nile and we proceeded to Rakesh's house where comfort and rest awaited us. It was early afternoon when we reached the house with the hot Egyptian sun beating down on us. I wanted to show Richard around Cairo, but he wanted to rest. I took him to my room and closed the balcony doors to shut out the bright sun as he lay on the bed.

"Do you need anything, Richard?" I asked, kissing his forehead.

"Some water, I'm feeling parched."

"Stay here and rest," I whispered, "I won't be a moment."

I procured a pitcher of water from one of the servants and headed back to Richard. As I approached the room, I heard him speaking to Madame Duchamp. Not wishing to disturb them and to satisfy my own curiosity, I lingered just outside the door and listened as Madame Duchamp spoke, "Drink this, Richard, it is a mix of different herbs that will help you regain your strength."

"Thank you, Madame Duchamp. Actually, I did want to speak to you alone," he confessed.

"What is on your mind?" she asked.

"Christina told me everything," he began, "I just wanted to thank you. I know without your help, I would not be here."

"Christina's Power is very strong, Richard, but she required the proper guidance to use it. What she did was very dangerous and despite my warnings and objections, she wanted to do it regardless of the consequences. Her mind was made up, so I prepared her as best I could and thankfully both of you returned. Christina loves you and has risked everything for you; continue to keep her happy and that is thanks enough."

"I love your daughter and will do anything for her."

With that, I decided to enter the room and was relieved there was no animosity between them. I gave Richard his water and kissed his moistened lips.

"Let Richard rest now," Madame Duchamp suggested, "you can see him later."

As I closed the door behind us, I felt her hand on my shoulder.

"Was what you heard to your liking?" she smiled.

"What do you mean?" I asked, feeling my face flush.

"I knew you were outside the door," she admitted, "what was it you expected to hear?"

"I wasn't sure," I nervously replied.

"You are hiding something," she sensed, "tell me, Christina."

"I thought you harbored some resentment toward Richard," I confessed as we walked down the hall.

"Whatever would make you think that?" she sounded hurt.

"I know that you were against the whole idea of my going to free him . . ." I began before she stopped me and declared, "My concern was for your safety, I did not want to lose you. Richard is the nephew of one of my dearest friends and your lover, I have no ill will toward him."

"I am sorry, Mother. I thought you perceived him as a distraction."

"Your desire to learn has always been strong, Christina," she commented, "now that you've seen what the Power can do, I think you will be an even more dedicated student."

"What more have you to teach me?" I curiously asked.

"Come," she smiled and I followed her down the hall.

We met Rakesh at the front door and walked out into the busy streets of Cairo.

"Your mother told me your Power is very strong and from what I have witnessed in the Temple of Set, she is correct," Rakesh stated, "You have outwitted the Lord of the Dead and returned unscathed – something not easily accomplished. The time has come for you to use your Power's full potential, you have done well but you can surpass even your own expectations."

"How?" I was intrigued.

"By imposing your will upon others," he answered with a smile.

"How is that possible?" I curiously asked.

"Your will drives your Power, Christina," he explained, "Just as you can manipulate the elements, you can control another's will."

"Tell me," I pleaded.

"Channel the Power through your eyes," he instructed, "the eyes are a powerful source of energy and emotion and once the Power is directed into the eyes of another, the will is easily manipulated."

I was anxious to employ my newly acquired knowledge but I wanted to first see how it worked.

"Can you do that?" I asked Madame Duchamp.

"Of course," she smiled as she looked at Rakesh, "who do you think taught me?"

"Will you show me?" I pleaded.

She took me by the hand and we walked toward the marketplace where a merchant had a small table of jewelry. "Pick something," she offered. I pointed to a small silver ring as Madame Duchamp stared into the merchant's eyes. No words were exchanged between them, just a glance that only lasted a few seconds. The merchant handed me the ring that I had pointed to and when I offered him money, he declined with a wave of his hand. "That's how it works, Christina," she whispered as she ushered me away from the table. "That was just a simple demonstration, once you manipulate someone's will, there is nothing you can't make him or her do," she explained.

As we wandered through the marketplace, I noticed a man in Egyptian attire following us from a distance. I said nothing to Madame Duchamp or Rakesh who had not seemed to notice the pursuer. He seemed to be watching me mostly but I could not figure out why, so I devised a plan to confront him myself.

I told Madame Duchamp I wanted to go to the perfume and oil marketplace and I would meet them back at Rakesh's house in one hour. She was reluctant to let me go on my own, but I simply told her, "The Power has served me well and continues to protect me."

"My instincts tell me that you are up to something, Christina," she presumed.

"Trust me," I confidently replied, "as I have trusted you."

"Very well," she relented, "one hour."

I thanked her and headed toward the oil and perfume market where I was sure the intruder would follow. My assumption was correct, for he was still on my trail as I wandered through the marketplace gazing at the oddly shaped bottles of scented oils. I saw him out of the corner of my eye, cautiously watching my every move. An old mosque stood at the edge of the marketplace, damaged by fire and abandoned some time ago from the looks of it. I decided it would be here that I would confront my pursuer and uncover whatever plot he was hatching. I cautiously entered the deserted building and lay in wait behind a pile of rubble to see if he was brave enough to enter. Moments later I heard the footfalls of an intruder carefully enter and begin to quietly search for his quarry. I held my breath as he neared the pile of rubble that kept me out of sight and when I was sure he was past me, I silently emerged from my hideaway and crept up behind him, almost close enough to touch him and mockingly asked, "Have you lost something?"

He quickly spun around with a look of fright that gave way to anger as he announced, "I saw what you did at the jewelry merchant's table, you are one of Set's minions!"

"I did nothing," I protested, but he was adamant.

"Set's evil light burns within you and I will extinguish it as my sword pierces your heart!" he proclaimed as he drew a long sword from beneath his cloak and started toward me but abruptly stopped as my eyes met his. I stared hard at him as I felt the Power ignite behind my own eyes and I could actually *see* what I wanted him to do. The Power had enabled me to peer directly into his soul and seize his will, absorbing it into my own.

I said nothing more to him but he completely understood what I demanded of him. He took his sword in both hands and with my nod of approval thrust the blade deep into his own heart.

"*Keep your eyes open,*" I said to him in my thoughts, "*I want you to see death as it takes you.*"

The blood spurted from his heart and ran down the smooth blade as he crumpled to the floor with eyes wide open in complete obedience. The rush of his life force hit me hard as I felt my pulse quicken and my Power grow stronger. It took a few moments for me to catch my breath and regain my composure, but the stimulating feeling that lingered was more potent than any opium high and it was genuine. I walked out of the abandoned mosque one life richer and my newly acquired knowledge put to the test.

9

I was true to my word and met Madame Duchamp back at the house within one hour.

"Christina," she smiled as she approached me, "your eyes are ablaze with the Power, you've killed, haven't you?"

"I have," I excitedly replied and proceeded to describe my encounter with the would-be assassin.

"You absorb knowledge so quickly," she complimented, "and your confidence is much improved."

"I have you to thank for that, mother," I said embracing her, "your knowledge and Power have no equal and you have been patient with me even though I have not always deserved it."

"I've watched you grow from a naïve child to a confident adult," she replied, "and you have made me proud. You've learned much of the world and its workings and have manipulated it well, but . . ."

"I still have more to learn," I concluded.

"Yes, you do," she smiled, "but tonight we celebrate. Rakesh is preparing quite a lavish affair for us."

After everything I had been through, a party would be a welcome reprieve. I went back to my room and prepared myself for the evening while Richard continued to sleep.

As soon as I was groomed and attired, I heard Richard wake and call to me.

"Did you sleep well?" I asked, kneeling beside the bed.

"You look beautiful, Christina," he said stroking my cheek.

"All for you," I modestly replied, "Come now, you must get up and prepare for tonight's celebration."

"But I've nothing to wear," he protested as there came a knocking at the door. I sprang to my feet and opened the door to find Rakesh with an assortment of garments over his arm.

"Forgive me," he apologized, "but I thought Richard would prefer something more becoming for a young Englishman to wear."

"Thank you, sir," Richard replied astonished, "but how did you . . ."

"I will see both of you downstairs," he smiled as he turned to leave. Richard eagerly rose from the bed and readied himself as I waited.

Before long he stood in front of me, refined and handsomely attired.

"May I escort you to the banquet hall, Mademoiselle Lafage?" he sweetly asked.

"I would be delighted," I beamed, taking his arm.

I could hear music as we made our way to the banquet hall, the steady pulse of drums quickening my footsteps. As we entered, both of us marveled at the amazing display that lay before us. The room itself was decorated with brightly colored silks and wall hangings accentuated by radiant candlelight. The long table was lavishly embellished with an array of exotic foods that smelled as appetizing as they looked. There were several guests crowded around the table – Egyptians, Europeans, and a few Turks – all delighting in the feast that lay before them.

We feasted and drank with them as the musicians from Rakesh's café provided the atmosphere for the evening.

"Richard, you're looking much better," Madame Duchamp observed as she and Rakesh approached us.

"Thank you, Madame Duchamp and may I say you look beautiful this evening," he replied as he kissed her hand.

"It's nice to have you back, Richard," she replied in earnest.

"Rakesh, I want to express my gratitude for everything you have done for me," Richard sincerely declared.

"Your happiness and enjoyment are thanks enough," he imparted, "now enjoy yourselves!"

The sweet smell of opium wafted toward us as my eyes met Madame Duchamp's and the four of us proceeded to the far end of the hall where a small number of hookahs were smoldering with the blissful narcotic. As we sat before the tentacled device, I asked Richard if he had done this before.

"Only once," he replied, "my uncle took me to an opium den in London, it was quite an experience."

As we smoked, I told Richard about the afternoon's events regarding my encounter in the abandoned mosque and how I was able to force my pursuer into suicide. He responded with a gentle kiss, the sweet taste of opium lingering on his lips.

"You are a deadly beauty, my love," he commended.

I winked at him as we continued to inhale the dreamy narcotic from the bubbling hookah. I felt the opium take me as I began to notice the dazzling colors and the swirling music as my senses began to tingle. I looked at Richard and could tell from his eyes that his senses had also surrendered to the hypnotic opium. He took me by the hand as we watched the musicians perform and admired the blaze of brilliant color that seemed to radiate from everywhere.

"Come with me," he whispered as he led me up the marble staircase and back toward the room we shared. He opened the balcony doors and bid me to come hither. "Look," he dreamily directed my eyes upward at the shimmering stars in the night sky.

"It's beautiful," I gasped as his lips began caressing my neck. I closed my eyes in ecstasy as the sensation of his kisses permeated my entire be-ing. I kissed him intensely, my tongue caressing his, still tasting the sweet smoke of the opium as his hands slid down my shoulders, peeling off my gown. He wrapped his arms around me, lifted me up and set me down on the edge of the balcony. He stripped off his shirt as I undid his trousers and wrapped my legs around him, allowing him to move smoothly inside me. The seductive rhythm of his body inflamed my appetite for him as his thrusts became quicker, sending us into a raging climax. I tossed my head back and savored the pleasure, whispering his name and embracing him tightly.

"You are a more potent narcotic than any opium," he asserted, his chest heaving.

"You are quite addictive yourself, many nights I've longed for your touch," I confessed.

"Long no more, I'm here for you," he said with a long, deep kiss.

I licked his lips and smiled, still tasting opium and pomegranate juice.

"Do you want to go back downstairs?" he playfully asked.

"I suppose we should," I smiled, "Rakesh did go through a lot of preparation for this evening."

We rejoined the party, still going strong with guests, food and the sweet aroma of opium amid the swelling rhythm of the music. I met many people that evening, some clients of Rakesh, for whom he had performed various spells and others who were followers of the forbidden worship of Set. I hadn't realized how far and wide Lucien's empire extended until Madame Duchamp had explained that there was no place on earth where Lucien did not have a devoted following.

"From the great cities of Europe to remote and far away countries such as Egypt, the Master's Power has endured and will continue," she proudly stated.

The party slowly began to wind down as the guests thanked Rakesh for such a magnificent evening. Dawn was on the horizon as we bid farewell to the last guest and retired to our rooms for a long rest.

10

The time we spent in Egypt was the happiest I had ever been and the memories will stay with me even after my ashes have been scattered to the four winds. Weeks went by as Richard's health returned and he once again resembled the man I had met at the Paris opera. We spent our time exploring Cairo and the pyramids, making love in the ruins of great temples and enjoying spectacular entertainment at Rakesh's café.

One morning as Richard and I were admiring the sunrise, I heard footsteps coming down the hall and a knock at the door.

"Enter," Richard politely hailed as Madame Duchamp entered the room.

"I need to speak to both of you," she began as she joined us on the balcony.

"What is it, mother?" I curiously asked, although I had a sense of what she wanted to say. Since rescuing Richard, my training had been on somewhat of a hiatus and it seemed it was time to get back to work.

"Richard, you have made an excellent recovery and this has proved to be a restful holiday for us all, but it is time to return to France. More mysteries of the invisible world await your discovery, Christina, as well as opportunities to strengthen your Power."

"I hate to leave here," I said, looking down at the dusty streets of Cairo.

"It is quite beautiful," she replied, laying her arm over my shoulders, "but we must go."

As much as I did not want to leave Cairo, I knew she was right and I wanted to continue to learn all she had to teach me.

"When do we leave?" I reluctantly asked.

"In two days," she replied. "It will be springtime when we get to France, at least we've escaped the winter," she mused.

"I would like to return here someday," I confessed as the Muslim call to prayer drifted toward us.

We did as much as we could over the remaining two days -- revisiting the pyramids and ruins as well as the marketplace and Rakesh's café. It was at the café where Rakesh had arranged a farewell party for us the night before our departure.

"I hate to see you go," he admitted, "but after you learn everything your mother has to teach you, maybe you will return. You are always welcome here."

"Thank you, Rakesh. You are a most gracious host," I commended.

The morning of our departure came all too quickly as we prepared to board the ferry for Alexandria. I noticed a strange box that I had not brought with me was about to be loaded onto the ferry.

"Wait," I said to the porter, "that is not mine."

"Go ahead and load that box," Rakesh ordered from behind me. "That is a gift from me, Christina," he conceded, taking my hand. "I think you know what it is. Now have a safe journey and may Set watch over you."

"Many thanks, Rakesh, for everything you have done for us," I sincerely replied and as he let my hand go, I felt something in my palm. It was a small leather pouch filled with tiny brown balls of opium.

"Now you know what is in the box," he smiled.

I thanked him again by offering him a hug and a kiss on the cheek. Madame Duchamp and Richard said their farewells to Rakesh and we were on our way down the Nile to the busy port of Alexandria. We were able to board a ship for France not long after arriving in Alexandria. The ship would make its usual stops in Greece and Naples before docking in France. The weeks aboard the ship were much more tolerable than they had been going to Egypt. I was still bored, but the anxiety and restlessness had not returned and I was able to share the beauty and wonder of our stopovers with Richard, who seemed as intrigued as I was at seeing these cities for the first time. Our journey home had passed without incident and as the carriage pulled up in front of the house, I felt a sense of relief at being home and on dry land.

Babette cheerfully greeted us at the door and reported that scores of clients had been anxiously awaiting our return. She was a bit shocked at Richard's appearance and nearly fainted when he stepped out of the carriage.

"I. . . I thought you were . . ." she stammered.

"He was," Madame Duchamp interjected, "but as you can see he is very much alive and will be staying with us."

"As you wish, Madame," she quivered.

"Richard," Madame Duchamp said to him, "stay with us as long as you want. My home is yours."

"Thank you, Madame," he replied as he embraced her, "I am truly grateful."

"Are you all right, Babette?" I asked as I entered the house.

"I have seen many strange things in my years of service to Madame Duchamp," she declared, "but I have never seen the dead live again."

"That was not an easy task and it nearly cost me my life, but it was worth it," I explained and smiled as Richard walked through the door.

"I'm sorry if I frightened you, Babette," he warmly apologized.

"Think nothing of it, Monsieur, I am at your service," she replied, less fearful, "Your Power is truly remarkable, Mademoiselle Lafage."

My instruction in the Black Arts resumed as we settled back into life as we knew it before our Egyptian sojourn. We were inundated with clients whose requests ranged from simple potions to complicated death spells. I watched and worked with Madame Duchamp as she guided me and increasingly let me perform spells on my own. My Power increased, feeling stronger than I had ever felt it, my confidence growing along with it. No longer did I have the feelings of doubt or failure that had plagued me months ago.

All the fears I harbored had vanished and it was with determined self-assuredness that I rose early that spring morning to gather mandrake plants for a particularly strong love potion I was to concoct for a loyal client. I quietly rose, gently kissed my sleeping lover's lips and crept into the hallway. The house was still, I had the morning to myself to welcome the morning sun's rays as I opened the door and headed for the forest where the mandrake was plentiful. It was still early enough where there were not many people around as I walked to the outskirts of the city and into the wilderness beyond. The warm sun on my face and damp grass beneath my feet created a feeling of serenity as I began to pluck the mandrake from the earth.

I was not in the field long when the serene feeling melted into an uneasy one and I began to sense a malevolent presence. I quickly spun around to catch sight of a hand as it was put to my forehead with such force that I was incapable of stopping it. It had begun draining my Power and I felt myself quickly getting weaker before crumpling to the ground as Abaddon stood over me and sneered, "We had a deal, Mademoiselle Lafage."

I looked up in shock into his glowing eyes that had now burned more intensely with my Power.

"Abaddon," I gasped, "how did you find me?"

"I'm flattered you have not forgotten me," he sarcastically remarked, "I have bided my time with you, Mademoiselle Lafage and I have not forgotten. I told you that you had reminded me of someone and after that stunt you pulled, I remembered one who had deceived me so many years ago. You resemble her a great deal, you are her offspring, are you not?"

"I know not whom you speak of," I firmly stated.

"Don't lie to me, Christina," he growled as he drew near to where I lay in the grass, his fetid breath hot on my face. "You see, a man recently came to me who was hanged for heresy in England. His mistress also had an appointment on the gallows, but he begged for her life, begged me to intervene and spare her life. I visited the magistrate in a dream and convinced him to show leniency and allow her to live. This man, I believe you know him as Sir James Ridgewood, swore allegiance to me in exchange for his lover's life. So I asked him, 'Where might I find Christina Lafage?' and this may offer you some comfort, it seems he thinks very highly of you and your mother. He was reluctant to tell me but I reminded him of the bargain he had struck and what might happen to his mistress if he did not comply. He told me everything, Christina, so you see there is no reason to lie."

Rage burned within me but I had not the power to fight against him. "You have taken my Power, what more do you want of me?" I angrily asked.

A devious smile spread across his face, "Oh, I have plans for you, fair maiden, and you shall have all of eternity to spend in my service. Your mother deceived me and I vowed revenge, now I have you both – you without your Power and she without her daughter."

I cringed as he put his hand around my neck and whispered, "I could snap your neck right now."

"Then do it and be done with me," I spat back at him.

"No, Christina, that would be much too easy, too quick. I want you to be aware of your approaching death. I want you know the exact hour, agonizing as the minutes drag and the anxiety gnaws at your insides."

I heard footsteps coming closer as Abaddon backed away from me and triumphantly stated, "I have sent someone for you and I will expect you soon at the gateway of the dead."

"Abaddon, you bastard!" I shouted as he faded into the wind with a devious laugh.

"Christina Lafage!" a man's voice shouted as he approached with two henchmen beside him.

"I am she," I sadly confessed, rising from the grass.

"Christina Lafage, you are under arrest for heresy and murder," the sheriff announced as he placed shackles on my wrists and ankles and led me back toward the city.

I was paraded through the city streets as people shouted obscenities and spat on me. I hated them all and wished them all dead, including my captors, but without the Power, all I could do was wish.

We entered the courthouse where I was led down a long aisle, filled with rows of spectators and thrown in front of the magistrates.

There were three of them in all; the one that sat in the middle, a man named Roget, spoke first, "Christina Lafage, you are accused of heresy, murder and blasphemous acts. What have you to say?"

I looked at him hatefully, a fat old man who wore a loathsome scowl on his face. "Who accuses me?!" I demanded to know.

Who could Abaddon have recruited to put his plan into motion?

"Bring out the accuser!" barked Roget.

An English sheriff emerged from the magistrate's chambers shoving Rebecca, Sir James' mistress, in front of him. She looked at me with tears in her eyes and she wept, "Christina, I am so sorry."

I felt so betrayed but I was determined not to show them tears and I held nothing but contempt for Rebecca as she stood in front of the magistrates.

"Mademoiselle Lafage, do you require a lawyer?" Roget asked.

"Would it matter? Since I am as good as convicted in the eyes of this court," I abruptly stated.

He looked at me with contempt and bellowed, "Let the record show that the accused refused counsel!" "You will state your name for the court records," he commanded, looking at Rebecca.

"Rebecca Tyler" she wept.

"And what acts have you seen Mademoiselle Lafage perform?" he interrogated.

"I have seen her use her Power to kill an English magistrate named William Moorsgate. She called forth demons to rip him into pieces and then cursed his spirit to wander the earth. She has also told me of others she has killed with her evil Power."

"Now then," he barked, looking in my direction, "you will answer to these charges and any other questions put to you by this court. Failure to answer will result in torture until you do answer. Do you understand?"

"Yes," I hissed.

"Do you deny these allegations, Mademoiselle Lafage?" he continued.

"I do not," I proudly answered. I knew the penalty for heresy and sorcery was death, but I knew I was already convicted before I even set foot in the courthouse and I had no desire to be tortured. Knowing I would never see Richard or my mother again was torture enough and I fought hard to hold back the tears.

"How long have you walked the left hand path?" Roget continued his interrogation.

"About one year," I responded.

"How is it you came to walk this blasphemous path?" the second magistrate, a man named Lemere asked.

I did not wish to implicate Madame Duchamp, so I told the magistrate that I was approached by Lucien and he bestowed the Power upon me.

"Was there an oath?" he roughly asked.

"Yes, I renounced your church, surrendered my soul and swore allegiance to my dark prince in exchange for knowledge and the Power. I have mixed potions, performed death spells, and I have raised the dead. I have taken my master into my soul as well as my bed."

The audience in the courtroom gasped and crossed themselves as I complacently answered the court's questions.

"Have you no remorse for your actions?!" Nogent, one of the other magistrates angrily shouted.

"None!" I defiantly replied, "I have served my master well."

"Then why does he not help you now?" the fat magistrate sneered, "Why not use your Power to save yourself?"

"My Power was taken by a demon that I had tricked. The same demon Rebecca Tyler struck a deal with!" I shouted and pointed to Rebecca. "The same demon that spoke to the English magistrate in a dream and convinced him to spare her life!"

"You dare accuse an English magistrate of bargaining with demons?!" the English sheriff roared.

"Sheriff Stratton," Roget spoke, "do you wish to take Mademoiselle Lafage to England to stand trial for the murder of William Moorsgate?"

"That will not be necessary," he replied, "she has already confessed to the murder, let her own people see her executed. I will bear witness for the English authorities."

"Very well," he nodded and then directed his gaze toward me, "It seems your master has forsaken you and your service to him has been for nothing."

"I know not what motives my Lord has," I insolently stated, "do you ever question your lord?"

"I have had enough of your arrogance!" Roget screamed as he slammed his fist down on the bench and then announced, "Christina Lafage, this court finds you guilty of murder, heresy and sorcery. The court hereby sentences you to hang by the neck until you are dead and that your body be burned until there is nothing left of you but ash and bone!"

Seething with anger, I spat at the magistrates and shouted, "You will regret this!"

As the sheriff led me down the aisle, the audience in the courtroom clapped and cheered as a bell tolled in a muffled tone proclaiming the death sentence of a heretic. I was once again paraded through the streets of Paris, this time as a convicted heretic and led to the Bastille, where I would be held until dawn when my sentence would be carried out. The drawbridge was slowly lowered as we approached the Bastille whose lofty towers loomed in the morning sunlight.

A gangly, unkempt guard came to meet us as my escort explained, "This is Christina Lafage, she is to die tomorrow morning."

"What was her crime?" the guard gruffly asked.

"Sorcery, heresy and murder. She is to be hanged," the sheriff replied.

"Come with me," said the guard as he ushered me to one of the cells in the seven-story tower of the Bastille. The door was unlocked and I was shoved inside an octagon shaped room that consisted of a bed, two chairs, a table and a stove. The guard closed the door and much to my horror, threw me down on the bed tearing at my clothes. With the shackles still on my wrists, I could not fight back as he undid his trousers and forced himself on me. I started to scream but he quickly put his hand over my mouth and finished his foul business. I was enraged, I wanted to kill him so bad I could taste it, but without the Power I was helpless.

"Such beauty should not be wasted," he smiled as he undid my shackles.

I lunged at him and struck him on the jaw but he quickly overpowered me and threw me to the floor.

"Some powerful sorceress you are," he laughed as he left my cell and locked the door.

The grim reality of my situation had finally descended upon me as I sat on the bed and began to cry. I truly was alone. Richard and Madame Duchamp were not here and I had no way of telling them where I was and it seemed Lucien really had abandoned me. How could he betray me after I swore allegiance to him?

"Lucien, why have you allowed Abaddon to do this to me, your loyal servant?" I cried.

I heard a key unlock my door as the guard announced, "You have a visitor."

I was astonished to see Rebecca, who entered the cell with tears in her eyes. "Christina, I am truly sorry, but the English authorities spared my life on the condition that I tell them who killed William Moorsgate. They killed Sir James and the other members of the London Hellfire Club, it was horrible."

"So you gave us all away to save yourself!" I shouted.

"I had to, I did not want to hang!" she replied.

I sprang from the bed and wrapped my hands around her neck, squeezing the life from her and cursing her as I did.

The guard, hearing the commotion, burst into the cell and separated us before I could carry out my task.

"I shall watch you hang tomorrow!" she choked as the guard escorted her from my cell.

So here I sit, composing this narrative with the rats as my only companions as the sunlight fades and tears fill my eyes. Tomorrow I will die with no regrets and no remorse. The Power is an amazing gift and despite what has happened to me, I would gladly surrender my soul again for the chance to wield it.

I do perhaps have one regret, that being unable to say goodbye to Richard and my mother, the only people who have ever meant anything to me. I will miss them both and carry them with me in my heart even beyond the grave. I still do not understand why Lucien has abandoned me but perhaps he can answer that when I see him in Hell, where I am sure to spend eternity.

11

And so Christina Lafage closed her diary on what she thought would be her final entry, unaware of the shadowy figure lurking behind her as she wrote her last lines.

It placed a hand on her shoulder and whispered, "I have not abandoned you, Christina."

"Lucien," she said in awe as she stood to face him, "Why have you let this happen?"

"I have not let anything happen, Christina," he scolded, "I did not force you into the Land of the Dead. You have tricked the trickster and paid the ultimate price . . . all for love of a mortal."

"I do not expect you to understand," she replied defensively.

"I understand many things," he stated, wiping her tears, "especially your reverence for the Power and your willingness to use and expand it. I have been monitoring your progress and you have impressed me a great deal with your abilities and the speed at which you learn them. It seems such a shame for you to die so young with so much potential."

"I do not wish to die, but to continue in your service," she conceded.

"Give me your left hand," Lucien commanded as he unsheathed a small dagger. Christina willingly complied, looking into Lucien's dark eyes as he made a clean slice across her palm and then his own. He pressed their hands together and as their blood transfused, Christina felt as if a bolt of lightning had struck her, electrifying her whole body. The force of energy was so great, she could barely breathe as her eyes rolled up and her body trembled with the immense Power that flowed through her. As their hands separated, Christina was thrown to the floor gasping for air and her heart pounded fiercely as the Power flowed through her like a raging inferno.

"Rise, Christina," Lucien commanded as he stretched out his hand and pulled Christina to her feet. "You promised to serve me and serve me you have. Your Power is restored, more potent than you could ever imagine. My blood flows through your veins and your Power can never be taken again. I am a part of you now as you are a part of me."

"What do you ask in return?" she panted.

"Your continued service and that you leave the dead in their rightful place, it is not for you to decide who is to be given another chance."

"I understand, Lord, and thank you," she replied, kneeling before him and bowing her head.

"Come here," he whispered and took her hand as she rose, licking the blood from her wound and kissing her deeply.

"Use your Power to leave here as soon as night falls," he advised.

"What of Abaddon, am I strong enough to defeat him?" she eagerly asked.

"Abaddon will trouble you no further," Lucien replied, "he is my concern and I will deal with him."

Christina was somewhat disappointed she could not avenge herself but she knew whatever Lucien had in mind for Abaddon would be far worse than anything her newly-restored Power was capable of.

As Christina waited for nightfall, Madame Duchamp and Richard were beginning to worry, as they had not seen Christina all day.

"I know she must have gone to gather mandrake, but she should have returned by now," Madame Duchamp declared with deep concern.

"I will go look for her," Richard volunteered, "I'm sure she just lost track of time."

"I hope you are right, Richard," she nervously replied.

"You don't think something could have happened, do you?" he asked with a slight quiver in his voice.

"I know Christina's Power is strong enough to keep her out of any danger, but something just doesn't *feel* right," she confessed.

"Don't worry," Richard assured, placing his hands on her shoulders, "I will find her."

"Christina, what has happened to you?" Madame Duchamp whispered to herself as she paced the floor of the parlor, "if I only knew."

She suddenly realized that she did possess the means to find Christina as she quickly ran to the kitchen and went down into the cellar where the crystal ball sat on the long table. She closed her eyes, took a deep breath and began to concentrate, but something distracted her. She opened her eyes and was startled to find Abaddon on the other side of the table.

"Looking for someone?" he slyly asked.

"Abaddon!" she gasped.

"It has been a long time, hasn't it?" he reminisced with a smile, "And vengeance never tasted sweeter."

Madame Duchamp's fear quickly turned to red-hot anger as she angrily shouted, "What have you done with Christina?!"

"I vowed revenge and I have not forgotten, Madame," he calmly stated.

"I should have known your foul hand was in this. Where is my daughter?!" she angrily demanded.

"In the Bastille, awaiting execution for murder and heresy," he smugly replied, "I have taken Christina's Power and saw to her apprehension and death sentence, and now I pronounce sentence upon you!"

Abaddon lunged at Madame Duchamp but her Power had thrust him back and slammed him into a wall of shelves, shattering bottles of herbs, propelling shards of glass in every direction.

"Possessing the Power is one thing; knowing how to use it is quite another!" she chided.

"You are an arrogant woman!" he growled.

"And you are inexperienced!" she shot back as she commanded the broken glass to spear Abaddon, causing the demon to shriek and become enraged. With his eyes glowing an intense, almost blinding red, he mustered his strength and rage and once again charged toward her, but this time she was not able to stop him as he seized her by the throat, pinning her against the damp wall of the cellar.

"Ah, but I learn fast!" he exclaimed, "And taking your life will be a pleasure!"

The quick glint of metal from a hatchet lying on the table caught her eye as she stared hard at it, causing it to take flight and sever the claw-like hand that clutched her throat. The blood spurted forth in a rushing stream of red as he fell to his knees, clutching his bloody stump.

"My life is not so easily taken, Abaddon!" Madame Duchamp affirmed as she removed the severed hand from her throat and threw it toward him.

"You will pay dearly for that!" he growled, slowly rising to his feet and staring straight into her eyes. "Come to me!" he demanded.

Madame Duchamp found herself advancing toward Abaddon despite her resistance and unwillingness to let him defeat her. She tried hard, but could not break free of his commanding power. He licked his fangs as she drew closer to him, unable to resist the fire in his eyes that seemed to suck the very life from her. He bent her head back, exposing her neck throbbing with her blood and Power.

"Your Power will make me even stronger," he whispered, but just before he could sink his fangs into her warm flesh, a voice boomed from behind him, "ABADDON!"

He quickly turned to see Lucien with a whip in his hand and rage in his eyes.

"Master!" he exclaimed as he let Madame Duchamp go and dropped to his knees.

"I have given you no permission to leave your domain, why do you defy me?!" Lucien roared, uncoiling the whip and bringing it down on Abaddon with a loud crack.

"Please, Lord," he begged, "this woman and her daughter have deceived me; I will take their Power and their lives and have my vengeance."

"Power is not yours to administer, *I* decide who deserves the Power!" Lucien forcefully asserted.

"I want my vengeance!" said Abaddon, quivering in Lucien's presence.

"I grow tired of your insubordination, Abaddon!" Lucien growled as he brought the whip down on him several more times until the demon was writhing in pain on the stone floor. "Return to your domain!" Lucien commanded, "And trouble this woman and her daughter no more!"

"As you command, Lord," Abaddon whimpered as Lucien sent him back to the Land of the Dead in a bright flash of fire.

"Thank you, my Lord," Madame Duchamp warmly thanked him.

He approached her and touched her cheek, "I could not allow Abaddon to take Power from two of my most faithful servants. I have been to see Christina and I have restored her Power."

"So what Abaddon told me is true," she gasped.

"Christina's Power will enable her to escape," Lucien assured, "go to her now, she will need you."

"We will continue in your service, my Lord," she pledged as she knelt before him.

"I will see both of you soon," Lucien promised as he pulled her up and kissed her.

Madame Duchamp ran upstairs and ordered Babette to have a carriage discreetly waiting near the Bastille. As Babette left to carry out her mistress' orders, Richard burst into the house and announced, "Madame Duchamp, Christina is locked in the Bastille! She was tried and convicted . . . "

"I know," Madame Duchamp broke in and proceeded to tell him of Abaddon and Lucien's visit. "Night is falling now. We must go!" she shouted, grabbing a red velvet bag and handing Richard a loaded pistol.

"What about you?" he asked, taking the pistol and hiding it under his coat.

"I am armed with the Power," she proudly replied, "nothing will stop me!"

The dark night had descended upon them as they reached the lofty gates of the Bastille.

"How will we escape with Christina?" Richard whispered.

"Right through the front gate," she answered.

"But the guards . . ." he said, bewildered.

"Don't worry about the guards, leave them to me," she replied, looking into his troubled eyes, "trust me, Richard."

She looked around and saw a carriage waiting across from the Bastille accompanied by Babette, who had caught Madame Duchamp's glance and discreetly nodded.

"Let's go," she said to Richard as they approached the guard stationed in front of the immense prison.

"We wish to see Christina Lafage," she announced.

"At this time of night?" the guard asked, agitated. She stared straight into his eyes and commanded, "You will let us in, now."

12

The darkness that Christina had waited for had finally fallen. As she planned her escape, she heard a key unlock her door and turned to see the guard who had raped her enter.

"Well, sorceress, since this is your final night with us, I would like the pleasure of your company one last time," he mischievously smiled.

"You will not touch me again," she snarled.

"Oh, won't I?" he mockingly laughed, drawing his sword, "You will do as I say or you will not die a quick death by hanging, but rather a slow and painful one at the end of this sword!"

Christina stared at him hatefully as she concentrated on the Power and directed it at his sword. The sword began to vibrate and the guard dropped it in horror and ran toward the door of the cell, but it abruptly slammed shut.

"Leaving so soon, monsieur?" Christina mused, "Don't forget your sword."

The sword launched itself at the guard but stopped just before piercing his heart.

"Mademoiselle, please . . ." he whimpered as the cold blade touched his chest.

"Don't worry, monsieur," Christina assured, "the blade will not even touch your heart."

"So what they said about you is true, you do possess the devil's Power!" he nervously stammered, "Please, I . . . I could help you escape, but in the name of God don't kill me!"

"God?" she angrily questioned him, "Was it this God you called upon when you forced yourself on me and threatened to kill me?!"

"Mademoiselle, please!" he cried.

"Stand over by the window," she commanded.

As he moved toward the window, the sword followed, still pointed at his fiercely beating heart. The guard was sweating profusely as he waited for Christina's next move.

He stared at the sword and then back at Christina, who smiled and announced, "As I have said, monsieur, the sword will not touch your heart."

The sword began to back away from the guard's chest as he breathed a sigh of relief, but before he could relax any of his tense muscles, the sword flew back toward him and made a clean cut across his abdomen, spilling his intestines onto the floor at Christina's feet. The guard released a bloodcurdling scream and his eyes widened in horror as he glared at his own entrails hanging from his open belly.

"We are not done yet, my friend," Christina smiled as she directed her Power at the sword and as she looked up, it followed her gaze and imbedded itself into the stone wall just above the window. The guard lay at her feet in his own blood and viscera, but still alive.

"Get up!" she commanded as her Power raised the guard to his feet. She stared at the pile of entrails, commanding one end to wrap itself around the sword and the other to coil around the guard's throat. "The people of Paris will not see me hang, but they will witness a hanging!" she vowed and hurled her Power toward the guard, forcing him out the window to hang helplessly by his own entrails. A bright light blasted through the window and hit Christina like an arrow, rushing through her body and intensifying her Power.

Two guards, roused by the frightful scream of their comrade, rushed into Christina's cell and were horrified by the grisly scene they encountered. Christina spun around to face them with a wicked smile on her face and fire in her eyes.

One guard dropped to his knees and made the sign of the cross, while the other drew his pistol and shouted, "I will send you straight to hell myself where you belong!" His finger squeezed the trigger and Christina quickly raised her hand as the bullet sped from the pistol and abruptly stopped as it hit Christina's wall of Power and fell to the floor.

She gazed into the guard's startled face as the other guard shouted, "Don't look into her eyes, the fire of hell burns within them!"

But he was too late; Christina had silently transmitted her command to her unwitting pawn and his will became hers. She smiled as he drew his sword and silently said to him, *"Now!"* The guard swiftly and forcefully swung his sword, neatly severing the head of his kneeling comrade before plunging the sword into his own belly. Christina stood in the middle of the cell, spattered with blood, absorbing the life force of the two fallen guards at her feet when Richard and Madame Duchamp rushed into her cell.

"Christina!" Richard shouted as he ran toward her. The guard who had escorted them gasped in terror at the slaughtered remains before him and nervously drew his sword. Richard heard the sword slide from its scabbard and whirled around as he drew his pistol and fired, hitting the guard squarely in the chest.

"You've done well, my love," said Christina as she embraced Richard.

"Anything for you, Christina," he replied, gently kissing her bloody lips.

"Come you two, we've no time to waste," Madame Duchamp broke in as she reached into the velvet bag and pulled out the mummified Hand of Glory that they had fashioned so long ago. Its wizened fingers still grasped the candle that Madame Duchamp now lit as she recited,

"Hand of Glory, cast your light,

Burn on through the night,

May sleep linger over this place,

With no guards able to give chase,

Grant safe passage for us three,

Over land and across the sea."

Christina squinted at the bright light emanating from the macabre talisman as she protested, "I did not wish to make my escape this way, I want to take as many lives as I can so the people of Paris will feel my wrath!"

"That is a much too reckless display of Power, Christina," Madame Duchamp chastised, "Causing such a riot in the Bastille will make our escape most difficult."

"They sentenced me to hang!" Christina shouted, "They paraded me through the streets like a common peasant!"

"It is not wise to let anger and emotion make such rash decisions," Madame Duchamp advised, "it is better to be discreet than extravagant. Let the citizens of Paris sleep anticipating your execution. It will be a greater shock when they discover that you have escaped."

"But I want to make them suffer!" Christina cried as her hands clenched into tight fists and blood trickled down her palms.

"You are letting your wounded pride get the best of you," Madame Duchamp observed, "Let it go."

Christina backed down, although she was filled with rage but memories of what had happened between her and Madame Duchamp the last time her rage had gotten control over her flooded her mind and she did not want another confrontation like that again.

"It's not worth it, Christina," Richard said in a comforting tone, "don't let it destroy you."

She took a deep breath and relented solemnly, "Let's go then."

"I understand how you feel, Christina," Madame Duchamp said as she took Christina by the hand, "but part of mastering the Power is knowing when to show restraint."

"I know," Christina softly answered, "but I have such a fiery rage burning inside me and it is difficult to extinguish it once it has been inflamed. I. . . just need to release it, I can't keep it inside me."

"You are so like your father," Madame Duchamp professed as she touched Christina's face, "He never believed in restraint and let his emotions govern his actions. Don't fall into that, Christina, it will ruin you. Come, I know it is difficult, but walk away."

Christina swallowed hard as she took her mother's hand and with great difficulty left her wounded pride with the mutilated guards in her cell.

"The guards and the prisoners will sleep until the Hand of Glory is found and extinguished," Madame Duchamp explained, "by that time we will be far away from here."

"Where will we go?" Christina asked as the three of them made their way out of the tower where Christina was held.

Madame Duchamp just smiled and said, "I think you will be pleasantly surprised when we get there."

The entire prison was quiet while they slipped past the sleeping guards and through the gates of the Bastille unopposed. Richard and Christina climbed into the carriage with Babette as they observed Madame Duchamp whisper something to Gerard, the driver. She entered the carriage and sat silently with eyes closed and in deep concentration.

"What's happening?" Richard whispered.

"I. . . I don't know," Christina answered, perplexed.

Madame Duchamp continued to linger in a deep meditative state as the carriage traveled the deserted Paris streets until it came to a halt outside the courthouse where Christina had been convicted and sentenced.

"Why have we stopped here?" she angrily demanded to know.

Madame Duchamp suddenly came out of her trance-like state and looked at her daughter with a mischievous smile and replied, "Come with me."

"I don't want to be near this horrible place," Christina protested.

"You have nothing to fear, Christina," Madame Duchamp responded, "come with me."

Christina was reluctant, but she trusted her mother and followed her out of the carriage.

"Wait for us around the corner," Madame Duchamp instructed Gerard and took Christina's hand, leading her into the courthouse.

"Why have you brought me here?" Christina asked as the doors of the courthouse opened, revealing Roget, Lemere and Nogent, the three magistrates who presided over Christina's trial. They seemed to be in utter confusion as to why they felt compelled to come to the courthouse in the middle of the night but it became clear to them as soon as they saw Christina and Madame Duchamp standing in the doorway.

"The devil has summoned us here!" Nogent shouted as he turned a ghostly white.

"I can't give you all of Paris, Christina," Madame Duchamp triumphantly stated, "but I can give you the three men responsible for your peril. Do what you will with your prey, my daughter."

"Thank you, Mother," she smiled as she walked toward the three men in front of the judges' bench.

"Well," she proudly began, "it seems that my master has not abandoned me; he has in fact greatly rewarded me."

She directed her gaze up to the huge stone gargoyles that adorned the pillared walls of the courthouse and silently commanded, "*Serve me.*" The courthouse was filled with a low crumbling sound as three of the gargoyles extracted themselves from the wall that faced Christina. Their stone feet hit the floor with a heavy thud and their eyes glowed a fiery red as they walked past the magistrates and knelt in front of Christina.

"You will burn in eternal torment for your evil deeds!" Nogent shouted.

"You have much to say," Christina mockingly declared, "too much for my liking." She looked down at her kneeling minions and touched the cool stone head of the gargoyle to her right. "Silence him!" she commanded. Her stone servant rose to his feet and with heavy steps moved toward the trembling magistrate. He was paralyzed with fear as he opened his mouth to scream, but before sound could escape his lips, the gargoyle thrust his stony hand into the mouth of the terrified magistrate, ripping his tongue from his mouth with such force that it sent Nogent sprawling to the floor in a growing pool of blood.

Roget, the head magistrate, seemed unaffected by what he saw as he arrogantly asked, "Why have you summoned us here?"

"Please, mademoiselle," Lemere interrupted with quivering voice, "I beg you to spare our lives."

"Stop groveling, you coward!" Roget chided. "If you are to kill us, Mademoiselle Lafage, do it quickly and get it over with!"

"No!" Lemere shouted as he ran down the aisle toward the door.

"Stop him!" Christina commanded as the gargoyle kneeling directly in front of her rose and hurled himself at Lemere, pinning him against the wall with his stone horns.

"Don't kill him yet, my pet," Christina taunted as the gargoyle's stone horns began to pierce Lemere's heaving chest.

"As for you, Roget, I will kill you and I assure you it will not be a quick death," she vowed, "nor a pleasant one." Filled with confidence, she moved toward Roget and peered into his eyes. "Tell me, what frightens such a righteous man like you, Roget?"

"*You* certainly do not frighten me, Mademoiselle Lafage," he snorted.

"Ah, but I see something that does frighten you," she triumphantly stated, "hot and brilliant as it crackles and burns, filling the air with acrid plumes of smoke."

Roget's face turned a deathly pale as his brave façade began to crumble.

"No one knows my fear of fire," he gasped.

"Your brother was horribly burned and later died in a fire when you were both children, since then you have had an all-consuming fear of fire. There is nothing you can hide from me," Christina smiled, then nodded to the gargoyle on her left. "Sit his eminence down on his esteemed bench." The gargoyle carried the magistrate to the wooden bench from where he had convicted Christina and sentenced her to hang. It stood behind Roget, firmly holding him on the bench as Christina picked up a lit candle and approached him. Roget shuddered as she put the candle to his face, "I could simply disfigure you. I could burn your face so badly that people would gasp in horror as they looked upon you, but that would not satisfy me. Your death will serve me much better . . . all of you!"

Christina placed the candle underneath the bench where her stone servant firmly held Roget. The wooden bench began to blacken as Roget squirmed under the stone hands that held him. "Squirm like the maggot that you are, Roget," Christina taunted as her lips curled into an impish smile.

"You think you have won?" Roget sobbed, "You have won nothing!"

"I have won my freedom and your life," Christina sneered, "and you are powerless against me."

"You will burn in the deepest trenches of Hell for this!" he shouted.

"I will sit at my master's left hand when my time on this earth is through," Christina declared, "as for the burning, I leave that to you."

Christina turned and walked toward the door where Madame Duchamp waited for her.

"Is this your final verdict, my daughter?" she asked.

"Not quite," Christina winked as she faced the magistrates and raised her arms, chanting,

"Rise, fire, rise

Reflect the fury in my eyes,

And in your bright blazing flash,

Reduce this foul place to ash!"

The walls of the courthouse began to glow a bright red, giving birth to sporadic flames that quickly spread, engulfing the courthouse in a matter of minutes. "Die slowly, gentlemen!" Christina shouted as she and Madame Duchamp made their exit.

"Has that satisfied your appetite for vengeance, Christina?" Madame Duchamp said as they descended the steps of the burning courthouse.

The light from the fire cast an eerie shadow over Christina's face as she replied, "Almost. There is one more stop I must make."

"We've not much time, Christina," Madame Duchamp remarked. "You must do it quickly. What is it that you still need to do?"

"I want Rebecca Tyler," Christina gravely replied as flames ravished the courthouse behind them.

Rebecca Tyler was sequestered at an inn not far from the courthouse. She lay in bed, unable to sleep, anticipating the next morning's events. Rebecca convinced herself that she would rest easier when Christina Lafage had met her demise.

"Don't worry," Stratton, the English sheriff, had told her earlier, "Christina Lafage is locked away in the Bastille and cannot harm you."

But his words did little to comfort her. After all, Christina was justified in her resentment toward Rebecca and she was fearful that Christina would curse her from the gallows.

A bright light shone through Rebecca's window and she curiously rose from her bed to see where it came from. She looked out onto the darkened streets of Paris that had become illuminated by the fire coming from the courthouse. The courthouse! Rebecca began to tremble as she slowly backed away from the window and tears began to roll down her face. She was startled by a sudden knock at the door and her heart began to race.

"Rebecca, it's Sheriff Stratton!"

She breathed a slight sigh of relief as she opened the door and let the sheriff in.

"The courthouse is on fire and I'm told something strange has happened at the Bastille," he announced.

"The Bastille!" Rebecca exclaimed. "Christina Lafage has escaped, she's coming for me!"

"Christina Lafage is not going anywhere," Stratton firmly said, placing his hands on Rebecca's shoulders and trying to calm her, "she's under lock and key in the Bastille."

"No! I know she's escaped and she'll come here to kill me!" Rebecca cried.

"She's locked in a cell!" Stratton firmly replied. "Wait here, I will go to the Bastille to see what has happened and make sure she's in her cell."

"No!" Rebecca cried, "Don't leave me here alone, she'll kill me!"

"Stay here," Stratton replied, "lock that door and don't open it for anyone but me. I will be back as quickly as I can."

She closed the door behind him and locked it as he instructed but her body trembled with fear. She went to the window and impatiently waited for Stratton's return as the flames from the inferno at the courthouse lit up the night sky. She could hear shouts of men in the distance running to the blaze, trying to extinguish it, but she knew if Christina was responsible, the fire would rage until the courthouse was nothing but ash. She began to pray fervently and cursed the day she met Sir James and his wicked friends.

Rebecca looked out the window and through her mournful tears saw a solitary figure coming toward the inn. "At last," she sighed, "Sheriff Stratton has returned." Rebecca leaned out of the window as the figure abruptly stopped and raised its head. She gasped in horror as Christina looked up at her and maliciously smiled, her eyes glowing with vengeance.

"The magistrates are burning, Rebecca, can you not hear their screams riding on the wind?" Christina slyly asked, looking up at her frightened prey, "And now it is your time."

As Rebecca backed away from the window, she knew she could not escape Christina's wrath. She knelt down and resumed praying; asking for forgiveness and mercy that she knew would not be hers. She decided there was only one way to escape Christina as the tears came hot and bitter, streaming down her face and with trembling hand she began to write.

Christina entered the inn, where a crowd of drunken guests were on their way to see the inferno that raged at the courthouse. Christina approached the innkeeper, peering directly into his eyes and firmly asked, "In which room will I find Rebecca Tyler?"

"Room sixteen," he solemnly replied.

As Christina climbed the stairs, her hunger for vengeance was mounting with every step. When she reached room sixteen, she hurled her Power forward, ripping the door from its hinges and sending it crashing into the darkened room. She entered the room and a wave of disappointment washed over her as she beheld Rebecca's body hanging from a solitary beam in the ceiling, a noose fashioned from a bed sheet wound tightly around her neck. Christina was quick to notice a note pinned to Rebecca's sleeve addressed to her and ripped it from the hanging corpse. She lit a candle by the bedside and read, "I know that I will never be forgiven for the wicked things I have done and for the blasphemous acts I have witnessed, but I know what you had in store for me was far worse than death. I will see you in Hell, Christina."

Christina looked at her one-time friend in disgust and uttered, "How typical of you to take the coward's way out."

"Christina, are you here?" she heard Madame Duchamp's voice float into the room.

"In here, mother," she answered as Madame Duchamp walked into the room. "She hung herself," Christina gravely stated.

"She was frightened, Christina," Madame Duchamp said, putting her hand on Christina's shoulder, "she was too much of a frightened child to walk the path."

"She was a coward," Christina replied, still looking at the corpse in disgust.

"She was afraid of you, Christina," Madame Duchamp said as she turned Christina around to face her, "she witnessed what your Power could do when you killed William Moorsgate. She knew what you were capable of and chose to die by her own hand rather than endure a painful and torturous death."

"And it would have been so for her cruel betrayal," Christina declared, "I should have. . ."

"You are wasting too much energy on this. Focus your attention toward other things. You have me, you have Richard and you still have more to learn," Madame Duchamp broke in.

Christina sighed as she lowered her head as she came to realize her mother was right. There was no use lamenting what could have been, it was better to focus on what could be.

"The carriage is waiting outside, we must go now," Madame Duchamp said as Christina raised her head and embraced her, "Thank you, Mother."

"Let's go," Madame Duchamp smiled and took Christina's hand.

Christina turned around for one last glimpse of Rebecca and whispered, "May all the tortures of Hell be yours, Rebecca."

They crept down the stairs and outside to the waiting carriage and quickly climbed in.

"Is everything all right, Christina?" Richard asked as Christina fell into his arms.

"Yes," she answered, squeezing him tightly, "I love you, Richard."

Madame Duchamp knocked firmly on the roof of the carriage and called out for Gerard to drive. Gerard took hold of the reins and yanked them gently as the horses broke into a gentle gallop down the deserted street into the welcoming arms of the night.

Christina Lafage and her companions were not seen again in Paris after that night. Some say they headed east, others say they boarded a ship and sailed north. But whatever direction Christina's destiny took her, her legend continued to grow and stories of Christina Lafage continued to be told in whispers on the dark streets of Paris.

About the Author

Eve Lestrange lives in a quiet New Jersey suburb where haunting dreams and visions often visit. Eve has always been drawn to writing - first to poetry, then short stories and finally to novels. She mostly enjoys writing horror stories that take place in a historical setting, as she has a deep interest in history and archaeology.

Made in the USA
Middletown, DE
04 September 2017